Behold!

Book One of the Soul Reader Series
A Novel By
J. Don Wright

For Virginia, who always believes.

And for Betsey, who helped make it all come true.

ONE

"SURE, I'M LOOKING FORWARD to my first day of high school, mom," Priscilla said from her wheelchair by the garage door. "Just like I looked forward to the 37 corrective surgeries the doctors said would improve my mobility and dexterity."

Priscilla Benson maneuvered her motorized wheelchair by sipping and puffing into a tube positioned in front of her mouth. Her head was the only part of her body over which she had control.

"Honey, I know you're bitter, and you have every right to be," Marrisa Benson responded. "But remember what the psychologist said, *You can make the best of your bad situation...*"

"Or you can make a bad situation the worst," Priscilla completed the sentence.

She'd heard it enough times it no longer held any meaning for her. She couldn't help but notice her mother's aura, which was usually bright blue with some peach edges, now had definite muddy, dark blue swirls in it. She had learned, since she'd begun seeing people's *colors* shortly after the accident, that muddy colors meant trouble or turmoil.

The love and pity in Marrisa's eyes was obvious, but so was the underlying steel. She would be damned if she would allow her once-vibrant daughter to become a morose, churlish stranger.

"So, when I pick you up from school, are we still on for pizza?" she asked, trying to lighten the mood.

"Mom, I love you, and I love that you want me to be happy, but I don't want to go out anywhere in public. Criminy, I don't even want to go to school, even if it is a Friday, and only for one day," she finished with emphasis.

"Criminy?" Marrisa mimicked questioningly. Pris watched as some of the muddiness in her aura diminished.

"I've been reading about merry old England in the 17th century," Pris replied.

Marisa just shook her head and smiled. At least her daughter's wicked sense of humor was intact, if a little jagged.

"SO, READY TO JOIN THE freaks and geeks club?" asked a voice from behind her.

Turning the chair around required her to sip or puff gently into the control tube for right or left movement. Pris had already practiced, and was prepared to launch into, a blistering repertoire of insults directed at anyone with full use of their body. Facing her was the grinning visage of a slightly-build, freckled, red-haired boy about 13-years-old; in a motorized wheelchair. His aura was bright, blazing red with a darker red border and golden halo. His was the most beautiful aura she had ever seen since she had awakened to the ability after coming out of the coma from the car wreck.

"You...I...what..." Priscilla stuttered, causing the grinning boy's smile to make a concerted effort to split his face in two.

"Oh, great, you're not just crippled, you're a moron as well," he quipped. "Oh, well, beggars can't be choosers," he observed with feigned resignation. "There's an orientation for ADA students, all five of us, in 10 minutes in the counselor's office. Come on, I'll show you the way," he offered, driving around her on the wide sidewalk and moving off without hesitation or backward glance.

"I'm not a moron," Pris shouted after the retreating figure, then concentrated on directing her chair to follow. "I may be slow, but I'm not that kind of slow," she muttered under her breath.

The bad part about her blow chair, as she thought of it, was that she couldn't yet talk and steer simultaneously. She often quipped in conversation how the same limitation should be a law for anyone driving a car, especially under 30 years old. She had tried a chair which was guided by a plate positioned in her mouth so she used pressure from her tongue to direct it, but was dismayed at how soon her tongue tired. When her tongue had ultimately cramped as she tried to force the issue, she knew it wasn't for her.

"Thanks," she called in between breaths to a tall boy who held the sliding door for her. She had seen the automatic door plate on the wall and was headed to hit it with the rubber fist attached to the front of her chair. Her tormenter had already entered the building and the door was starting to close. The tall boy smiled and nodded before moving off to join a waiting group of other gangly, awkward teenagers.

She hadn't seen a violet aura like his before, and she sat in the doorway staring after him several seconds. The automatic door trying to close on the wheel of her chair brought her back from her musings, and she turned down the wide, locker-lined hallway. Hamilton was just turning the corner ahead, but Priscilla's chair only had one speed; slow. She complained incessantly to her mother about needing a faster chair.

"Mom, it takes forever to get from one class to the next, which makes me habitually late," she said, sounding just like a Valley Girl. "Which in turn makes everyone look up when I rattle in and disrupt the classroom, and then my mood just spirals down from there."

"Sweetheart, I know how much better it would make your life," Marrisa replied with a long-suffering expression. "And I know how important your mobility is to you, but we'll just have to wait until the finances will allow it. I've spoken with the supervisor at a local medical supply company and he understands, as his son is also wheelchair-bound."

She smiled ruefully, but the tears were visible at the corners of her eyes. "He says he's working on getting you a demonstration model that's two years old, as soon as the new model comes out. Apparently there's a waiting list of people in your situation who are asking for it and some of them are independent adults with no support system. I'm working every angle I can, okay?"

"It's all right, Mom, I'm sorry I complained. I know you're doing everything you can, and I love you," Pris replied softly.

Marrisa moved to her daughter's side, and hugged her fiercely. "We'll get through this, baby; you and me against the world," she whispered through clenched teeth. It was an old Anne Murray tune, but they had adopted it as their fight song.

Priscilla rounded the corner of the wide school hallway as Hamilton rolled into an office on the right, midway down the hall. When she arrived and slowly turned in, she was greeted with a too-small room filled with a desk, chair, and four wheelchairs with occupants. Hamilton was awkwardly turning his chair around to back into an open space on the wall, and the only room left was in the doorway.

"You must be Priscilla," the pudgy, bespectacled, middle-aged counselor standing behind the desk smiled warmly, rounding the corner to extend her hand. Today was a day for several firsts, Pris thought distractedly. She had also never seen a peach aura, especially not one with a deep purple fringe.

"Yes, I must be, otherwise I'd much rather be someone else," Pris quipped, allowing her acerbic tongue to cover for her momentary lapse in attention. "Sorry, I don't shake hands; I'm germaphobic. And besides, my hands don't work," she finished caustically.

"Oh, I'm sorry," the woman said quickly, jerking her hand back as if burned. "I haven't received your file, so I wasn't aware of your... status," she finished lamely.

"That's all right," Pris smiled insincerely. "The file is probably just like me; slow. Good ole' one-speed Prissy, that's me." She only referred to herself as Prissy when she was angry, and blasted anyone else who tried to use the name.

"Why don't we introduce ourselves?" the matronly woman hurried on. "I'll start. I'm Mrs. Delroy, and I'm the guidance counselor for all students with Access and Functional Needs. Troy, why don't you go next?" she continued, indicating a pasty-skinned, heavy-set youth with the beginnings of a goatee, sitting in the corner in a standard wheelchair.

"I'm Troy," he confirmed. "I'm the only sophomore, but we're all the same age. I'm kind of advanced for my age," he informed them. "But I'm not a Brainiac or anything like that," he hurriedly concluded.

He turned to his right and a mousey-haired girl who looked like she might have been six or seven years old. She was tiny to the point of frail and her arms and legs were stick-thin. She wore a shapeless, plain white smock over peach leggings, and sat in a joystick-controlled motorized chair.

"I'm Alice," she barely whispered in a little-girl voice. "Troy's right," she said, defiantly raising her head as if some inner voice had called her to attention. "I'm also thirteen. I have a version of Syndrome X; my body is growing much more slowly than my brain. I sometimes get headaches because my brain is too big for my skull. The doctor's hope my skull grows quickly, or I could develop aneurisms," she concluded.

Pris noted Alice's aura was an orangish-brown, with traces of grey streaked through it. *Just one more new set of colors I don't understand, from someone who apparently likes to over-share*, she thought.

Most of the kids she'd seen were run-of-the-mill blues and greens with the occasional orange or yellow. The teachers she had already met were either dark red, dark blue or purple auras; except for Mr. Jones the PE coach and assistant principal. His was mostly black, with a disposition to match.

"Tara," the next girl said bluntly, before cutting her eyes toward Hamilton. She was unremarkable physically, and sat in a regular manual chair. Her caramel-colored skin and high cheekbones didn't betray her lineage, and the only clue was the corn-rows pleated in her dark brown hair. Interestingly, her aura was similar in color to her skin-tone.

"I'm Hamilton," Ham informed them. "I like Fusion Jazz, slow strolls on the beach, and walking my dog *50 miles*. You can call me Ham, because I am, a bit." Pris noticed he smiled nearly all the time, and his aura sparkled through the spectrum of scarlet hues.

"You walk your dog 50 miles?" Alice asked dubiously.

"No, my dog's name is *50 miles*," Ham replied.

"Good one, Ham I Am," Troy chortled.

Even Mrs. Delroy laughed at that, but Tara, who had remained deadpan during all the exchanges, showed no reaction. Her golden-brown aura didn't ripple or pulse, it simply lay around her like a shroud. Pris could tell there was definite trouble in the young teen's life.

"Priscilla?" Mrs. Delroy said, turning toward her.

"I'm new to wheelchairs and the whole ADA routine, I'm easily frustrated and my chair is *slow*," she began. "I don't like fake people who pretend to care about helping me, and I can tell who is and who isn't. So that everyone knows, because most everyone already does; my dad and I..." her voice caught, and her pallor flamed scarlet. A brief look of rage crossed her otherwise slack countenance, and she took a deep breath. "My dad and I were in a car wreck 18 months ago and I spent 11 months in the hospital undergoing 37 unsuccessful operations. My father died."

The counselor broke the awkward silence after 15 seconds. "Very well," she said. "Let's get you all started on your class assignments and escorts."

She was handing out forms on clipboards as she spoke, but hesitated when she got to Hamilton. Reaching up with his one functional hand, he took the clipboard and tucked it neatly against his ribs, trapping it against the side of his chair. Fishing a pen from his shirt pocket, he made a show of studying the forms.

"Priscilla," Mrs. Delroy said, turning to face her. "I have a volunteer who will be here momentarily and she's been assigned to escort you around the first few days until you get used to the campus. Her name is Tiffany and she's a graduating senior."

Turning back toward the center of the room, she added, "All of you will have escorts available if you wish except Troy, who has volunteered to escort any of you who would like for him to do so."

"I'd like to go with Troy," Alice said immediately.

Mrs. Delroy looked questioningly at Troy and he smiled and nodded. "I'd be happy to show Alice around."

"Ham, Tara, would you like escorts?" the counselor inquired.

"I'd rather go with Priscilla, if it's all the same with you; and her of course," he added hastily.

All eyes turned to Pris. *How could he possibly know this is exactly what sets me off?* she thought. Beaming her most condescending smile, Pris said, "How could I possibly turn down such a gracious invitation from Ham I Am, especially when he wants to take care of me because he thinks I'm a moron."

"Oh, dear," Mrs. Delroy flustered, "we don't use terms like moron here, Priscilla. We prefer *mentally challenged.*"

"Well, I'm neither a *moron* nor in need of an escort so if we're through, may I go?" Tara asked caustically, flipping her clipboard onto the desk before wheeling herself away from the wall.

Mrs. Delroy jumped sideways out of her way but Pris simply sat staring at her for several seconds. Then slowly and deliberately, she sucked on the control tube to back her chair into the hall. The chair lurched as it traversed the low threshold and Mrs. Delroy lunged toward her involuntarily, concerned the chair might overturn.

Tara gave her wheels a vicious yank, pulling her hands in as her chair rolled neatly through the narrow space allowed by the doorframe. Snagging the left wheel in her gloved hand, she executed a sharp left turn before dropping her right hand onto the right wheel and speeding off down the hall.

A breathtakingly beautiful young woman walked up at that moment and Pris looked at her askance. *She's as beautiful inside as she is out*, she thought. The woman's indigo aura had a bright pink halo and her smile was just as radiant.

"Hi," the newcomer said, not offering her hand. "You're Priscilla and I'm Tiffany. Please don't think me flighty because of my name," she requested. "My mother is a huge Audrey Hepburn fan."

"Thank you Tiffany, for the introduction. My mother is an Elvis fan, so there you go," she countered. "Do you have a preference as to what you like being called, other than gorgeous?"

Tiffany blushed prettily and stammered, "I don't know that I've ever had a young lady call me gorgeous before, but I prefer Tiff."

"I was just saying out loud what Ham I Am and Troy are thinking," Pris replied with a saccharine smile. "In fact, any normal male between puberty and a hundred would be."

"Well, you're very flattering and ...bold, I guess is the right word," Tiff replied.

"Excellent," Pris responded. "This is my protector, Ham I Am; he thinks I'm a moron. Shall we go?"

TWO

"FOR THE LAST TIME, I do not think you're a moron," Ham whispered harshly. "And, I've apologized for saying so for the last time as well."

Pris had introduced herself to yet another person in the lunchroom as they waited for Tiffany to bring their meal trays. They had survived the first three periods without incident.

"I guess I'll have to forgive you, being as how we apparently have all the same classes," Pris responded. "I promise not to mention it again."

At the table next to theirs a noisy group of older girls were having a good time making fun of other, less-popular girls at the school. The topic of the welcome dance came up just as a short, thickly-built boy came over to their table.

"Candace," he began, addressing the obvious ruling queen at the table. "I was wondering... that is... I wanted to ask you if, well... do you have a date for the dance next week?"

"Bruce, Candy always has a date to any event at the school," the girl to Candy's right informed the interloper. Candy, for her part, waited until the other girls stopped laughing so her cutting remark could be heard by the maximum number of people in the crowded cafeteria.

"Bruce, the gimp at the next table has a better shot at taking me to the dance than you," she scolded.

Her aura was clearly visible to Priscilla. All the girls had similar shades of fluctuating red, orange and yellow, all muddied with black and gray swirls. Candace, on the other hand, had a bright violet aura with streaks of silver running through it.

A tempest of laughter erupted from the table and one of the girls rose from the queen's left, intent on further illustrating their disparaging opinion of the wayward suitor. As she stood from the round table, it appeared as if the loose flowing sleeve of her stylish fall blouse caught the corner of Candy's lunch tray. The tray contained a serving of spaghetti, a plastic glass of red fruit punch and an open container of applesauce. All three containers managed to empty their contents squarely into Candy's lap, right onto her startlingly white Muslin sundress. Candace's screech of humiliation and terror sounded like someone being attacked by a Great White shark.

"Clarice, look what you've done," the now soiled queen screamed. "You've ruined my two hundred dollar dress!"

Her aura had taken on a particularly greasy stain of blackish-green, ruining her image as completely as the spilled lunch had ruined her clothing. Candace leapt from the table, strewing spaghetti in a spray across the floor behind her as she whirled and ran for the restroom in the hallway outside.

Pris had watched the tableau unfold and had seen the look of rage flitter across Ham's face at Candy's cutting reference to him. She had also seen his right hand ball into a fist and jerk in the queen's direction. Ham's normally bright red aura had flared with striations of yellow and silver, making it look like a fiery sunset over the desert.

"Are you okay there, Ham?" Pris asked with sincere concern in her voice. When he turned his visage to her, the momentary stab of anguish in his eyes was unmistakable before shutters dropped over the pain and he smiled disarmingly.

"Why wouldn't I be?" Ham asked in reply. "That was the best demonstration of Karma I've seen since my neighbor ran over his son's bicycle. He didn't see it because he was too busy yelling at me for being in his way on the sidewalk when he came roaring into his driveway."

"We better eat up and get started toward your next classes," Tiffany said as she walked up to their table with three trays balanced in her hands. "What happened there?" she asked, nodding toward the melee still underway at the next table. The other girls, like a pack of feral animals, had turned on Clarise and were remonstrating against her clumsiness, stupidity, right to be in the group, and so on.

"Karma," Ham replied, digging into his spaghetti while Tiffany began carefully cutting up Priscilla's food into small bites before feeding them to her.

"Wow, waitress skills and understanding of quadriplegic eating habits," Pris observed benignly. "You're a regular Mother Theresa."

"You know, if we're going to be friends, you can drop the caustic routine," Tiff said neutrally. "You won't get any pity from me, and I'll only offer to do those things for you of which you're incapable."

Pris studied Tiffany for a long moment and nodded. "I guess I could use another friend," she allowed. "Now I have two."

Ham had wolfed down his meal and was backing away from the table as Tiffany collected their trays. "Gotta go empty the bag, meet you in class," he tossed over his shoulder.

"That sounds like a good idea, Pris," Tiffany observed. "Shall I check yours?"

Priscilla was torn between the embarrassment of a stranger handling one of her intimate needs and the desire to allow Tiffany to prove her previous statement. She decided as she was wheeling her chair around. "I'll meet you in the handicap stall near the front office."

"AS NEITHER ONE OF US died or killed anyone, I'd say our first day at the new school was a success," Ham was saying. They had rolled into the shade of a spreading elm tree while waiting for their parents to pick them up.

Most students were either headed toward or already aboard busses, except for those who had cars and driver's licenses, or friends with the same. A group of six boisterous older boys were gamboling across the campus toward the student parking lot and passed nearby. One separated from the group and approached them.

"Hey guys, check out the Hot Wheels," he called gleefully to his friends.

Priscilla sensed trouble immediately; his aura was mostly fiercely red, but darkened throughout by roiling black and gray blotches.

"Can I push you somewhere?" he asked Ham and Pris.

"We're fine thank you, we don't need any help," Priscilla answered as civilly as she could.

The bully wasn't hearing it. "Oh come on, my friends and I would be happy to help you. Hey Mike, grab the guy and we'll race," he suggested, moving behind Priscilla.

"Come on Butch, leave them alone," the one called Mike answered. "I need to get to work."

"She said we don't need any help," Ham ground out between clenched teeth. His right hand was fisted on his control plate, and trembled with suppressed rage.

"Well aren't you just the ungrateful type," the bully scolded. "Pete, grab Mr. Ungrateful and I'll race you to the car," he commanded another of the party.

Pris watched as Ham's fist twitched violently to the side and they all heard a sharp crack from above. All heads looked up just in time to see a large tree branch break and swing down directly at their assailant. Butch had no time to react other than to duck his head and the large branch hit him squarely in the back, sending him sprawling. The sprinkler system had been on earlier in the day and a puddle of muddy water stood in a low area a few yards away. Butch was hurled by the blow to land face first in the pool. His friends rushed to ensure he was unharmed and helped him limp toward their waiting vehicles. A horn sounded and Priscilla looked up to see her mother's van at the curb 30 feet away. A look of clear concern was on her face, but Pris pretended not to notice.

"I'm waiting with you until your ride gets here," she informed Ham. "I'm not leaving you alone in case those miscreants return."

"Miscreants?" Ham mimicked. "I don't have a ride," he said, changing the subject before Pris had a chance to lose a volley of derision at him. "I usually just roll home," he explained when she looked alarmed. "My dad often works late and he texted me saying he would be tonight. My chair has enough juice to make it home. This is all planned out. I've made the trip several times from my house to school and back during the summer so I know the way," he explained. "I'll see you Monday; have a good weekend."

"Wait...but...ah, can we offer you a ride home?" Pris stuttered, flaming because it was the second time in one day he had reduced her to stammering.

"I appreciate it but I don't think your van is equipped to secure two chairs," he reasoned. "Besides, I really like the neighborhood. It's fun to roll along and watch the world."

"Maybe I can *roll* home with you," Pris blurted out. She didn't even know where it came from; it certainly wasn't anything she'd thought through.

"Again I appreciate that, but we live in opposite directions," he replied. At her look of curiosity, he explained. "I checked out your address when Tiffany was filling out your registration sheet and I know the city pretty well. You live five miles from me that way," he said, pointing away from the school. "I live that way," he concluded, pointing over his shoulder toward the school. "I'll see you Monday," he said, turning his chair around to roll down the sidewalk back toward the school.

"Well how about dinner then?" she called back, trying not to sound desperate.

The retreating form stopped and his voice drifted back to her. "What's for dinner?"

"Mom and I are celebrating with pizza because some idiot in public education decided it would be a good idea to start school on a Friday," she called in return.

Ham turned around and rolled back closer. "Deep dish or thin crust?"

"The Pizza Piazza has every kind of pizza imaginable," Pris replied.

"*Does* your van have lock downs for two chairs?" Ham asked seriously.

"Mom will figure something out."

"Not necessary, my dad designed this chair," Ham shared. "It has its own lock down straps built in. All I need are three points to hook onto."

THE PIZZA PIAZZA DID indeed have every kind of pizza imaginable. It also offered a video arcade, Skee Ball lanes, and a huge assortment of activities and equipment for even the most finicky teenager; or adult. Marrisa loved to play Skee Ball but had chosen not to as Pris couldn't join in.

"Mom, go play; the relaxation will do you some good," Pris said emphatically.

"Oh, I feel like I'm abandoning you," Marissa replied.

Clearing his throat, Ham interceded. "Pardon my interjection, Mrs. Benson, but Priscilla and I have a great deal to discuss if we want to be ready for class on Monday. You'd actually be doing me a favor by allowing us the opportunity to talk at length about the future."

Marrisa looked from Ham to Pris, who nodded encouragingly. After another moment she did a little dance hop and skipped off to buy her tokens.

"That's the first time I've seen a mature woman actually skip," Ham commented.

"Who says my mom's mature?" Pris retorted.

"She's raising you by herself, isn't she?" Ham shot back. It took a moment of silence for the callousness of his comment to hit home and then he could only hang his head.

Pris just looked at him blankly. "What?"

After a minute longer Ham said, "I am so, so sorry. I didn't think about what I was saying. I only meant..."

"I know what you meant and it's okay," Pris replied gently.

"So why did you want to get rid of your mom?" Ham paused, blanching. "Wait, erase that. I can't believe I just committed two faux pas' in less than a minute. Why did you want to speak privately with me?"

"Will you stop being so sensitive?" Pris scolded. "I know you're not trying to hurt my feelings."

"You do?" Ham replied. "Oh, good, I'm so glad."

"Sure, you can't help it if you're a boy and by your very nature crude, insensitive and boorish," Pris said sweetly, with a wicked twinkle in her eye.

Ham's head came up and his eyes sparkled as well. Then he grinned and they both burst out in unfettered laughter. Each time the laughter began to die down, they would lock eyes and it would start all over again. After five minutes, when the laughter began to take on a hysterical edge and they were finally able to stop, Ham looked at her and said simply, "What?"

Suddenly serious, Pris said, "I think you caused the lunch tray and the tree branch to happen."

Ham turned his head at an odd angle and looked at her as if studying a rare and fascinating alien life form. "Do what?" he asked.

"You heard me," Pris replied.

"You're not making any sense."

"Of course I am; I was watching, you weren't," she corrected. "In fact on both occasions, I witnessed you balling up your fist and jerking it at the troglodytes in question; just before the *accidents* happened."

"That's crazy talk," Ham replied.

"We can test my theory," Pris suggested.

"And exactly how would we do that?" Ham asked.

"Said Troglodyte and crew just walked in the front door," Pris said, cutting her gaze over the corner of the booth.

Ham craned his neck around far enough to see them out of his peripheral vision. "They wouldn't dare try something in this crowd," he observed.

"Methinks thou dost misunderestimate the stupidity of the American jock," Priscilla snarked.

"Wait a minute; did you just butcher Shakespeare *and* quote George Bush, all in the same sentence?" Ham gasped in mock horror.

"You're so much quicker than you appear," Pris smiled.

"So, what's the plan?" Ham asked, enthralled in spite of his misgivings.

"I'm going to the service counter to sweetly inquire as to whether anyone might have the time to provide service to a pair of wheelchair-bound customers," Pris informed him.

"Ah, and you suppose they'll follow you back here?" he asked.

"Oh and here I just said you were quicker than you looked," She snarked.

"Well what then?" Ham asked impatiently.

"They'll watch where I go from a distance and fabricate some ridiculous plan which will seem brilliant to their feeble minds. We'll see right through it of course and thwart them, but not before you get the opportunity to get good and angry," Pris explained. "Then we'll get to test my theory."

"Hold on a minute," Ham cautioned. "Let's just say for the sake of discussion, because I don't have any mind powers, that I actually do. Won't demonstrating them here be a bit... awkward?"

"Well, silly man, the first two times you did it you made it look like it was an accident or someone else's fault," she reminded him. "I have faith your subconscious mind will work that out despite your conscious mind's reluctance."

"There's no talking you out of this, is there?" he asked hopefully.

"None whatsoever," she replied, with a wicked grin.

THREE

"YOU MADE ME LOOK LIKE a fool today," Butch hissed in Hamilton's ear. "Now it's gonna be your turn to get all wet and look stupid."

Ham and Pris had seen them separate at the front of the restaurant after holding a brief but animated discussion. Apparently, Mike still didn't want anything to do with it, because he had left the building. That hadn't stopped Butch from coercing or persuading his three lackeys to cooperate with his plan.

"Um, actually Butch, I had nothing to do with you getting wet," Ham tried in his most convincing voice. "The tree branch knocked you down. Did these guys not tell you that?"

"Yeah, they told me, but I know somehow you had something to do with it," Butch replied. Although by the confused looked on his face, even he was apparently struggling with the reasoning behind his conclusion.

"Look Butch, if you want to get even with the reason you got wet, maybe you should go water the tree?" Ham suggested.

Butch was a credit to most muscle-heads in that he actually thought the idea through for several seconds. Then he leaned in close to Ham's face and snarled, "Are you being a smart-ass?"

"No, not at all," Ham replied innocently. "I was just applying logic to our discussion. If you want to repay your getting wet with wetting something, and the tree is what caused you to get wet, then the tree should be your target. Unless you think maybe the sprinkler system is actually to blame as it was the source of the water. In that case, you could..."

"Just shut up," Butch barked. Heads turned from several booths around them and at least one employee stopped sweeping to watch what was transpiring.

If my power only works when I get mad this will never trigger it, Ham thought. *I'm having too much fun.*

"I'm done talking," Butch said and plucked a half-full pitcher of soda off an empty table. Holding it level with his face, he leered at Ham and said, "Let's see how you feel when your girlfriend is the one getting wet."

Extending his arm straight out from his side, he moved the pitcher over Priscilla's head. Then suddenly his arm bent at the elbow and he dashed the contents into his own face. He stood dazed for a moment, blinking to clear the stinging soda from his eyes. Then he held the empty pitcher out again and quickly bent his elbow, smacking himself in the face with the plastic vessel.

"Hey, stop," he yelled, as he extended his arm and smacked himself again, this time causing his nose to bleed. "Stop," he yelled again. "Make him stop." A third time he bashed himself in the face, this time hard enough to crack the plastic container.

His three goons had stood watching, stupefied, until Butch began yelling; then all three of them grabbed his arms and held him fast. Butch struggled and twitched for several seconds, then broke into sobs. His retinue helped him to the front door and they all went outside.

Pris had sat silently throughout the entire ordeal and now burst into gales of laughter. "That was amazing," she extolled. "Was that conscious or just suggestive?"

"Shh," Ham cautioned. "People are still watching us and they can hear you."

"Okay, roll over here and pretend to console me so we can talk quietly," Pris suggested.

Once their faces were less than a foot apart, Ham admitted, "I just thought; he doesn't realize he's really only going to hurt himself. Once he dumped a pitcher of soda on a girl in a wheelchair, he'd probably get expelled, kicked off the football team and maybe even arrested."

"So you just suggested the thought he was hurting himself and he actually did it?" Priscilla confirmed.

"So it would seem," Ham replied. "And it wasn't anything creepy like I was in his mind or seeing through his eyes. I just thought it and he did it. I wasn't even really thinking about him specifically. I was just waiting to see what happened if he actually dumped the soda on you."

"Wait, so you weren't trying to protect me?" Pris bristled.

"No, not consciously anyway," Ham started to answer before he saw the look on her face. "But as soon as I realized he was serious, I of course had to take drastic measures to prevent it."

"Sure you did, Buddy," Pris groused. "Sure you did."

Marrisa walked up to the table and paused briefly. "I'm sorry, were you two having an intimate moment? I can come back in a little while," she continued as she began to turn away.

"Mom, don't be ridiculous," Pris said sternly. "We just couldn't hear each other over all the noise and Ham moved closer so we didn't have to shout."

"Well, alrighty then," Marrisa said in her best *Ace Ventura*.

"So what did you win me, Mom?" Priscilla asked. Marrisa had been holding one hand behind her back since she had arrived. She now produced a small white plush horse with wings and a horn on its forehead. The wings were a glistening metallic blue.

"A pegacorn," Priscilla exclaimed.

"Pegacorn?" Ham repeated questioningly.

"Sure, silly man; a Unicorn with wings, or a Pegasus with a horn. Isn't it beautiful?" she breathed as Marrisa set it on the cross brace on the front of the wheelchair.

"Actually, it is quite... unique," Ham observed. But Pris wasn't listening; her eyes were locked on her prize.

IT HAD BEEN ON HER seventh birthday; her father had surprised her by bringing home a giant stuffed Pegacorn from a novelty store. She had fallen in love with it, and had sat on it for most of the remainder of the evening. It wasn't many days before her weight had buckled the legs to the point it became, in effect, a low cushion. After some cajoling, Pris had agreed it would best serve as her guardian while she slept, so it took up permanent residence at the foot of her bed. She had named it Fred.

After the accident, during the nearly a year Priscilla spent in the hospital undergoing reconstructive surgeries, Marrisa had sold their home and found an apartment with handicap access and amenities. Priscilla had finally been released from the hospital after the surgeons and specialists informed Marrisa there was nothing else they could do. Priscilla was shocked at her new home.

"Mom, why didn't you ask me if I wanted to move?" Pris had wailed. "I want my old bedroom back. I want my backyard swing set. I want my treehouse Daddy and I built. I want to…" She stopped abruptly, as recognition dawned on her that she would never swing, or climb trees, or even get upstairs to her bedroom without assistance. "I just want to be left alone for a while," she had finished.

Marrisa had left her alone for two weeks. At the end of that time they had the first of their many fights. "You don't have a choice, you have to eat," Marrisa had chastised Pris when she refused to open her mouth to be fed.

"Fix it where I can feed myself," Pris had demanded.

"You're being unreasonable," Marrisa had replied. "I don't even know if that's possible."

"Have you even tried?" Pris had shot back.

"Young lady, let me explain how it is to you," Marrisa had said crossly. "I didn't want to sell our home, I had to. Even after all the insurance payments from your father's company and the other driver's company, we still owed the hospital over 250 thousand dollars. And the surgeons waived a lot of their fees mainly because what they had hoped would happen; didn't. They offered to set up a payment schedule, but on my salary we barely have enough for expenses."

"How generous of them," Pris had shouted in fury. "They wrecked my body. I can't do anything except breathe and they waived their fees? We should be suing them for malpractice or something."

"Listen to me very closely," Marrisa had said then, becoming very quiet and moving very close to her daughter's face. "Those doctors saved your life. You were dead, for all intents and purposes. Your body was so badly mangled; they really didn't think you'd pull through." Tears had sprung into Marrisa's eyes, but she dashed them away and struggled on. "I begged them to try anything; unorthodoxed, untried, experimental. I couldn't bear to lose your father *and* you." And then she had laid her face in her hands and openly wept in front of her daughter for the first time.

Later that day Marrisa had told Priscilla about the storage unit. "Most of your belongings, including Fred, are there," she said. "We can get all the things you want to keep and sell or donate the rest."

When Marrisa had wheeled Pris to the roll up door in a borrowed wheelchair from the hospital, Pris had not been sure how she would feel. As the door went up, Fred was setting right on top of a stack of boxes in the middle of the small room. Memories of her father bringing it home and playing with her on it, and teasing her about never getting off of it, all came flooding back. Priscilla had hung her head and wept, finally allowing herself to truly mourn her father.

Once she was cried out, they talked about what to keep. "I don't think I can bear to have it around, Mama," Pris had admitted. "Every time I look at it I just want to cry again."

"IT'S TIME TO GET ON with my life and make the most of it I can," Pris had observed soon thereafter. They both agreed it was time for her to return to public school. Now she had a new Fred and a new friend and a new life, restricted as it may be. And she felt like the best might be yet to come.

"Have you notice how everyone steers a wide berth around us?" Ham had mentioned the second week of school. "It's like we're suddenly respected."

"More like either feared or loathed," Pris had responded. "I don't see respect in any of their colors," she finished absently.

"What do you mean their colors?" Ham inquired.

Oh, nothing," Pris tried to quickly dismiss her slip. "I mean their complexions. You know, if they were respectful they'd blush or show some sign of acknowledgement."

"Nah, I'm not buying it," Ham countered. "I've watched you with people for two weeks. You seem to be able to pick the friendliest, most trustworthy, reliable students on the campus. How is that?"

"I'm just a little empathetic, I guess," Pris deflected.

"Come on now, I've exposed my superpower, it's your turn," Ham chided.

"Okay," Pris sighed. "I can read people's auras."

"Sure, sure, you can...do what?" Ham stuttered. "You can read their auras; like their color signatures, you mean?"

"I don't know what that is, but I've researched enough to believe I'm seeing auras," she explained quietly.

They were parked under their favorite tree having gone outside into the pleasant afternoon air after another boring lunch. Ham had taken to feeding her and himself with his good hand and they were now seen as a couple on campus.

"So, what does her aura look like?" Ham asked of a passing girl.

"She's pretty, right?" Pris had observed.

"Sure," Ham acknowledged.

"Well, I've read enough now to interpret colors and she's a manipulative user who is afraid of something or someone here at school," Pris announced.

"How do you know all that?" Ham asked incredulously.

"Her aura is violet, not purple, with large gray masses in it and has a heavy black halo around it. Violet means persuasive, intuitive or visionary, but it can also mean manipulative," she explained. "The gray means she's afraid of or resisting something powerfully impactful in her life. And the black halo signifies she's either grieving or has a grudge against someone. I've watched how she is with boys and she uses her beauty and body to get them to do what she wants."

"Do you suppose the fear and grudge could have the same source?" Ham asked.

"I'm not that good at this yet," Pris admitted. "I'm still studying it and there are a lot of nuances in the process. I've also learned auras can change from time to time and even day to day if there's something powerful influencing a person's psyche."

"So you're psychic?" Ham asked with wonder.

"No, I don't think so," she replied. "I can't read minds or anything, I just see their colors. And something else I can't find any reference to; I can also see a glittering, bright area around everyone's heart. It's different for each person. Some are almost so bright they hurt my eyes, while others are dim or watery, like looking through cellophane."

"And you have no idea what that is?" Ham replied. "It's not something to do with their auras?"

There's no mention in any of the literature I have access to and I've read everything that even gets close to the topic," Pris assured him. "I'm still looking, but I really don't know what it is."

At that moment, an older man walked hurriedly past and Pris was shocked by what she saw. Her sharp intake of breath and the way it caused her chair to jerk was the only indication Ham saw, but he'd gotten to know her fairly well in the past two weeks.

"What is it?" he asked quickly.

"That man who just walked by; the older one?" Pris said, by way of identification. When Ham nodded, she said, "His aura is all black. I've never seen one *all* black. Even the really dark ones have *some* color. And his glitter?" she paused. When Ham nodded again she said breathlessly, "He doesn't have one."

"Excuse me," Ham called to a passing student who looked to be older than most. The young man hesitated, then walked back and stood before them. "Do you know who that older man is in the gray coveralls, going across the common?" Ham asked, pointing.

The student looked to where he indicated and said, "That's Mr. Jenkins, the head custodian. Nobody messes with him."

When he started to walk away, Ham asked, "Why not?"

Hesitating, the young man drew closer and spoke softly. "They say he killed a man in a fistfight when he was young. Beat him to death with his bare hands. They say he spent 30 years in prison. The school only hired him last year and a lot of the parents are telling the school to get rid of him. He scares everyone." At that, the young man turned and walked quickly away.

Ham and Pris looked at each other, startled. Could there be some connection with his glitter and his crime? Then the bell rang for the next class period. As they rolled toward the building, Ham said, "Oh hey, by the way. I didn't really think you had super powers, I was just teasing. Thanks for sharing with me, okay?"

FOUR

"I WONDER WHY THERE are police cars everywhere." Priscilla said as the hydraulic lift lowered her and her chair to the pavement. Ham had moved to the side of the van in the striped no parking area, to be there for her in case something happened. He knew there was little he could actually do but Pris felt better when he was there.

"Mr. Jenkins was murdered in his office Friday night, according to the rumors flying around," Ham informed her. "Or he was abducted by aliens and his lifeless husk was dropped back in his office over the weekend. I've heard both," he shrugged his one good shoulder.

"Isn't he the dark man with no sparkle?" Pris asked as Marrisa came around the front of the van.

"What did you just say, Priscilla?" Marrisa asked, having overheard her last question.

"Oh, I said he had no sparkle. You know, he just sort of shuffled around looking at the ground?" Pris answered, hoping her prevarication wouldn't catch up to her. "And he was always frowning like he was angry. You know; a dark personality?"

"Hmmm," Marrisa replied, uncertain whether to press the issue.

"We really should be heading to class as your chair takes a little longer than mine," Ham offered hopefully.

"I'll see you at four," Marrisa said to her daughter. The look on her face said he'd touched a nerve, but he didn't understand what.

"Mom, we have a Debate Club meeting after school, and it's not over until five," she reminded.

"Then I'll be right here at five," Marrisa promised. As she got in the van and pulled away from the parallel parking spot another man stepped from behind an SUV parked in the next space in the row.

"I need a few minutes of your time and I'll vouch for your tardiness," he said in a no-nonsense voice, simultaneously pulling his jacket off the front of his belt to reveal a police detective's shield.

"Of, course Detective, how may we be of assistance?" Ham inquired immediately.

Pris was once again impressed with how easily Hamilton maneuvered in the presence of strangers. She looked at the detective and smiled what she hoped was a friendly, cooperative expression.

"Your name is Priscilla?" he asked her.

Surprised, she nodded mutely but Ham was quick to respond. "Interesting how you already know our names, Detective...?" he paused inquisitively.

"Where are my manners?" the detective quipped. "I'm Detective Lieutenant Frank Kratos of the Chickasha PD; and your name, young man?"

"Ah, you overheard Mrs. Benson call her Pris and took a guess it wasn't a nickname but rather short for Priscilla," Ham guessed. "I'll bet you're really good at detecting. I'm Hamilton Nichols."

"Any kin to Martin Nichols, who works for Alert Medical Systems?" Frank inquired.

"He's my father," Ham replied quietly. The dark wings of misery which flitted for an instant through his eyes said he didn't really like being identified as his father's son.

Frank's expression took on a hooded look for a moment before he peered up from his notepad and smiled. "Your father does a lot of good work for the ADA community in Chickasha."

"And just how are you associated with *our* community, Detective?" Pris spoke for the first time.

"Mt wife is bedridden; has been for nearly a decade," he replied solemnly. "MS took her mobility at a young age." Returning his gaze to Ham, he continued. "Your father went out of his way to help the department get the very best medical equipment available for her condition, even when the insurance wouldn't cover specific models and features."

"Ah," Ham replied in understanding. "Yeah, he designed and had the factory custom build this model for me," he shared.

"So back to you, Priscilla; your last name is?" Frank asked politely.

"Benson," Pris responded. "I suppose you knew my father as well?"

Frank was quick enough to catch the past tense and his eyes clouded as he searched his memory. "Phillip Benson; his car was struck by a tractor-trailer after it jumped the median, three years ago. The truck driver had a massive heart-attack and was DOA. Benson was killed instantly and his daughter..." he stammered to a stop. "I'm very sorry Priscilla, I sometimes do that without thinking; hazards of the job. I read about all the surgeries you endured and the struggles you and your mother have suffered. I'm sorry for you loss," he finished in a whisper.

"You're very kind to remember," Pris offered.

"Yes well, I've had some little exposure to auras and I believe you have as well, haven't you?" he asked candidly.

"Ah, I'm not sure exactly what you're talking about..." Ham said, attempting to intercede, but Pris called him off.

"It's okay Ham, he's one of the good guys." She had been studying his aura and was beginning to understand she was in the presence of a rare human being, indeed.

"Tell me what you see Priscilla, if you would, please?" Frank asked.

"Magenta aura, bright reddish-purple, with beautiful gold and peach striations coursing through it. The aquamarine halo around it helps me understand how very special you are," she replied breathlessly.

"I'm having a good day then," Frank responded. "Clara says my peach doesn't manifest as often as I should let it, and the blue-green only comes and goes."

"Clara is your wife, I'm guessing?" Pris said.

"Yes and I tease her about it all the time," he smiled, "Clara the clairvoyant."

"But I'm not clairvoyant," Pris argued. "I just see auras. I don't see the future or tell fortunes, or read palms or Tarot cards..."

"Yet," Frank interjected. "After MS began to take portions of her mind, Clara developed unusual talents of being able to *see* and *follow* people anywhere within the greater city area. She's helped my with many of my cases and the department begrudgingly admits I'm not smart enough by myself to have the highest closing rate of any officer on the force."

"I'd love to meet her," Priscilla enthused. "I have so many questions."

"We can probably arrange that, but we'll have to wait for a cogent day," Frank explained. "Clara, unfortunately, can go for several days at a time unable to communicate even by grunting. And the next day she'll wake up, quite literally, singing." The look on his face spoke of how much he adored his beloved. Shaking himself as if he'd felt a chill, Frank returned to the business at hand.

"So tell me about Mr. Jenkins." It wasn't a suggestion; he was now all business.

When Pris got to the part about the sparkle it was Frank's turn to be in awe. The look on his face said all that was needed; his response verified it. "You see people's souls," he breathed.

"What?" both young people exploded simultaneously.

"Yes, my wife has described the ability as she learned about it from her mentor." Frank was almost effervescent. "An honest-to-God swami lived right here in Chickasha, Oklahoma until about five years ago when he passed away at a very old age. He used to come over and sit with Clara and I swear they were telepathic. They'd sit silently for the entire period, especially when Clara couldn't speak. And yet when she could, she'd tell me he was teaching her so much."

"But how do you know I see people's souls?" Pris insisted.

"Because you described it exactly the way Clara said Swami Maukra did," Frank explained. "A sparkling of bright energy, centered around the heart. Speaking of which; what a day of discovery, but let's get back to Mr. Jenkins. What was it about him you were saying when you got out of the van?"

"His aura was totally black and he had no sparkle," Pris confirmed.

"No sparkle meaning what; he had no soul?" Ham interjected. "How is that possible? Everyone alive has a soul," he stated emphatically.

"Actually according to Swami Maukra, there are many people who have no soul as we know it," Frank shared. "Clara says they lose it because they have no compassion, faith, or trust in humanity. They've been injured or damaged by an event, their environment, or society to the point their soul has been suppressed. They no longer exhibit, or at least not that any mystic can see."

"How many people can read auras or see souls?" Pris wanted to know.

"That's a good question Miss," Frank replied. "From most of the research Clara and I have conducted together, it's about one in 250 thousand for auras. The number is much larger in Tibet, India and parts of Pakistan. That may just be due to the higher exposure and number of mystical people available to point the way. Soul-readers are much rarer; they're not even a statistic of which I'm aware."

Pausing to reflect, Frank spoke again. "So if Jenkins had a black aura and no soul, it's possible he wasn't killed at all. Maybe he just gave up living. That would explain the MEs preliminary finding of natural causes."

"You mean he wasn't murdered or abducted by aliens?" Ham asked.

"The first part is inconclusive; the second, I can't speak to. That would be Sgt. Smithman, the desk sergeant," Frank supplied. "He's the X-Files fanatic. I suppose you two should get to class," Frank conceded. "I'll walk you into the office and vouch for you."

As they approached the building, Frank hesitated before deciding to forge ahead. "I think it best if we keep your talent from the general public, at least for now. There's no telling how many kooks there are out there and you're pretty vulnerable. I'll inform the assigned Resource Officer to keep an eye on you, but it's better if no one else know for now. I assume your mother knows?" he asked, looking straight into Pris' eyes.

"No, and I'm pretty sure she wouldn't believe me," Pris responded dejectedly.

"I'll wager I can be a big part of her accepting the truth," Frank offered. "Especially if she learns of it while accompanying you to my house for you to see Clara."

"Well don't worry too much about me," Pris said as Frank opened the door. "Ham is all the protection I need; he's telekinetic."

FIVE

"WHAT MADE YOU DECIDE to join the debate club?" Ham asked as they rolled toward the classroom where the meeting was being held.

"Really?" Priscilla responded. "Is there anything else I can do as far as after-school activities are concerned?"

"I guess that's right," Ham replied. "And I don't mind going along with you just to hear your wit and conversational skills exercised and honed," he added.

Priscilla cut him an inquisitory glance; she couldn't tell if he was teasing or not. She was beginning to get the hang of talking and turning the chair simultaneously while it was moving, but was still suffering through jerking turns and stops when she sucked too hard. Turning into the hall toward the classroom for their activity, her sudden intake of air caused the chair to rock to a halt. Ham stopped and pivoted his chair around. He looked at her inquisitively, and her eyes pointed to the end of the hall as her blanched expression told him she had seen something unexpected.

When she found her voice, Priscilla said, "I just saw Mr. Jenkins walk across the end of the hall."

"Mr. Jenkins is dead," Ham said.

"Do you think I don't know that?" Priscilla snapped. Without further discussion, Ham sped off down the hall. "Wait for me," Priscilla called after him.

Ham stopped abruptly, chagrined. "I'm sorry; I keep forgetting your chair doesn't go as fast as mine."

"I guess I'll just have to wait until the supervisor of the Medical Service Center can get me the display model he promised my mom," Pris replied.

"Oh," Ham exclaimed. "I didn't make the connection that you were the student in my school who was waiting on the faster chair."

"And what other student in our school needs a faster chair besides you and I?" Pris snarked.

"I thought it might have been Alice," he admitted.

Ham had begun moving down the hall again. As they rounded the corner where Priscilla had seen Jenkins disappear they were drawn to the sound of voices raised in heated argument. Approaching another classroom down a short hallway, they stopped shy of the door to listen.

"I don't care if they found one of the bodies," shouted the first voice.

"You have to care," shouted a second voice, just as loud.

"We have to stay on schedule," the first voice exploded.

"If we don't take a few days off and let things die down there won't *be* a schedule," shouted the second voice.

Ham decided to move a little closer, hoping to catch a glimpse of who was in the room without being seen. The two men chose the same moment to stop speaking and the whirr of his wheelchair was loud in the empty hallway.

"What was that?" the first voice asked in a more reasonable tone.

"I don't know, go check it out," gruffly replied the second voice.

Without thinking, Ham flicked his hand at the door and it slammed shut. Screwing up his face, he concentrated on the door lock. After a moment they both clearly heard the clack of the tumblers in the locking mechanism turning into place.

"Let's get out of here," Ham whispered fiercely, spinning his chair around.

Priscilla hard-sucked on the tube, commanding her chair to move backward. She was watching the convergence of the walls and hoping she didn't run into one before she reached the main hallway. She had never practiced backing long distances, but it made more sense to her to back down the short hall than take the time to turn around. The muffled sounds of shouting could be heard through the door as both teens continued their retreat. Ham had just turned the corner and stopped to look back for Priscilla when the distinctive spit of a pistol silencer was instantly followed by the crack of wood as the door splintered around the lock.

Backing into the main hallway, Priscilla soft-sipped to turn the chair left, then blew hard into the straw to move it forward. The drive mechanism complained at the abrupt change in direction but responded correctly. Concussions could be heard down the hallway behind them as one or both of the men kicked at the door, trying to force it open. Priscilla rolled forward just as the door jamb broke and the door crashed into the hall, rebounding off the wall behind it. She saw movement out of her peripheral vision as the hallway disappeared from her view.

Students from an earlier club meeting emptied out of a room into the hall-way, allowing Ham and Pris to gratefully blend into the crowd as it moved toward the exit. Flowing with the other students, they headed for the parking lot.

"I hope my mom is here early," Priscilla gasped between efforts to keep her chair moving straight down the sidewalk and talking. She was breathing so heavily from fear she was over-controlling the chair commands.

"If she's not, we'll have to stay with the other kids in the parking lot and hope your Mom gets here before they all leave," Ham replied.

Behind the group of students a short, heavy-set man with thick jowls and a bald pate stopped short of exiting the building. His rumpled suit hung open as he braced his arms over his head on the door frame, struggling to catch his breath. The grip of a pistol could be clearly seen under his left armpit. He glared after the group, not sure what to do next. Turning, he went back to the room where he and Jenkins had been arguing but the room was empty. Swearing an oath under his breath, he gathered his briefcase and cell phone before heading toward the rear entrance.

Having reached the parking lot within the relative safety of the crowd, Ham told Pris, "Stop here facing the parking lot."

"What are you going to do?" she asked; concern heavy in her voice.

"I'm just maneuvering around to face in the opposite direction," he said, stopping alongside her. "This way we can watch the front of the school and the parking lot simultaneously." Ham seemed overly proud of his quick thinking. "And this way if we have to move, you're already pointed in the right direction."

They sat in silence, allowing their breathing to return to normal. After several minutes Pris asked, "So your dad is the supervisor my mom has been working with?"

"Yeah and now that I know it's you, I'm going to push him to make it happen," he replied. "As soon as I can find him sober," he added quietly.

"Did your dad drink before your mom left?" Pris asked.

The expression in Ham's sorrowful eyes answered her. "Her leaving just seemed to break him," he replied dejectedly. "Don't get me wrong, he's still a good man and a good father, and he never abuses me; he's a happy drunk," he finished with a wan smile. "And he never goes to work drunk or drinks on the job," he added, seeming to want to assure her his father was dependable.

"So how long have you been able to lock doors with your power?" Pris asked, changing the subject.

"About 15 minutes, I'd say," Ham replied, glancing at his wristwatch.

"You mean you didn't know you could do that until you did?" she breathed.

"I just seem to be discovering more and more about my abilities, especially whenever you're around," he replied, unwilling to meet her eyes.

"What do you mean by that?" Priscilla asked warily.

"I mean, my powers have all manifested whenever I've felt like you were in danger," he replied, finally meeting her gaze.

"So, you're a protector then," Pris surmised.

"I'm *your* protector," he replied with thinly-veiled intent.

It was Priscilla's turn to avert her gaze. "I'm not sure how to respond to that," she said almost too softly to hear.

"Well, I guess you'll just have to get used to the idea that someone other than your mom cares about you," he stated matter-of-factly.

"We need to tell Frank what just happened," Pris blurted out after a moment, gratefully finding a way to change the sensitive subject.

"I'll do that when I get home," Ham replied. "He'll probably want to ask more questions, I'll bet. And here comes your mom. I'm okay with getting a ride home this time," he finished, and Pris just smiled.

SIX

"ARE YOU ABSOLUTELY certain it was Jenkins?" Frank asked Hamilton on the phone. Ham had called as soon as they were situated in the van; right after they'd told Marrisa. Doubt apparent on her face, she had approved when Ham insisted on calling the investigating detective.

"I didn't see him, sir," Ham replied. "Pris did."

"Does your phone have a speaker function?" Frank asked.

"Yes, sir, forgive me for not thinking of that right away," he replied. Looking at Marrisa, Ham said, "Frank wants me to put the phone on speaker." Marrisa nodded, pulling off the residential roadway into a small parking lot.

"You're on speaker, sir; go ahead," Ham informed Frank.

"Priscilla, how certain are you this was Mr. Jenkins?" He asked without preamble.

"I recognized him immediately because he had a black aura just like before, and no sparkle," she said, looking at her mom. She knew there would be more questions, but for now the police needed to know something very strange was afoot.

"As your mother is listening, I'm going to suggest you come over to my house as soon as possible," Frank replied. "That way we'll accomplish two goals at the same time."

"What two goals would that be, Detective?" Marrisa called from the front seat.

"Confirming what Priscilla saw and convincing you she sees what she does," Frank replied without hesitation.

Oh, Jiminy, Pris thought. *Talk about grabbing the bull by the horns.*

"And what exactly is it you think my daughter sees?" Marrisa inquired dubiously.

Rather than answer her directly, Frank decided on the logical conclusion approach. "Mrs. Benson, do you believe, as I am a police detective, that I'm a logical, reasonable man?" he asked.

"I'll give you that for now," Marrisa replied pointedly.

"So if I told you - as a logical, reasonable man - I had enlisted the aid of a psychic to help me solve over 20 unsolvable cases in the past three years; would you be willing to accept that as a premise?" Frank asked.

"I've read and watched television shows about such a concept, so I will say I don't immediately discard it as bunk," Marrisa replied.

"Excellent, I appreciate your scientific approach," Frank continued. "In theory all people possess undeveloped mental skills, with many often going through life without ever utilizing them. I believe the accident awakened those skills in Priscilla, and I believe I can persuade you to accept that by having you meet the psychic I've worked with."

"What makes you think by meeting a total stranger, one who claims to be a psychic, I would be more willing to accept this *awakening*?" Marrisa asked, doubt plain in her voice.

"Because the psychic I've worked with over the past three years I've also been married to for fifteen," he finished. "She, like Priscilla, had her abilities activated when Multiple Sclerosis crippled her ten years ago."

"CLARA IS HAVING A GOOD day then?" Ham asked Frank after the van pulled into the driveway of a sprawling ranch-style home. Large picture windows opened up onto the front lawn from two separate rooms. A neatly-manicured garden on the verge of the property would be clearly visible from the farther one.

"Yes, we had a nice conversation this morning and she's looking forward very much to meeting a soul-reader," he smiled from outside the open sliding door of the van.

Pris was lowering toward the broad driveway and Frank had opened the garage door, making access to the ramp into the house easier. A similar lift-equipped van was parked in the second slot.

"What exactly is a soul-reader, Detective?" Marrisa asked in confusion. She was trying to keep an open mind but this new term had her befuddled.

"As well as seeing auras, we also believe Priscilla can see a person's soul," Frank replied. "Before you get too wrapped up in the terms or titles, why not let Clara explain how all this works?" he cajoled. "She's far better at it than I."

"If I were a clairvoyant named Clara I'd change my name," Marrisa observed under her breath. "It sounds like a carnival routine."

When Frank cast Marrisa a sidelong glance she realized she had spoken too loudly. "No insult intended."

Trills of silver laughter pealed from the open doorway to the house. "None taken; by myself or Clara, apparently," Frank responded, nodding toward the sound of the laughter.

"How can she be laughing at what I said when there's no way she could have heard me unless she's right inside the door?" Marrisa wondered aloud. "I thought you said she was bedridden?"

"I also said she was a clairvoyant and a very powerful one at that," Frank smiled proudly. He led the procession through his house down overly-wide hallways and large, open arches. It was obvious the house had been built, or renovated, to accommodate wheelchair use. When they entered the room for which they had seen the second picture window, they saw a woman reclining in an elevated hospital bed. Her beatific smile and radiant countenance spoke of how happy she was to see them all.

"Priscilla," Clara said warmly. "Come here next to me so that I may touch you."

Obligingly and without hesitation, Pris did as requested. When Clara reached her hand out and laid it on Priscilla's arm, her eyes glowed as if backlit by an inner fire and a frisson of light and heat leapt between them. Pris had anticipated some reaction and had turned her head as much as possible away from the control tube. Even so, her sharp intake of breath caused the chair to quiver momentarily.

"Young lady, you have such a rare and special gift. We must work on helping you maximize your ability to use it," Clara said, as if the decision to do so were a foregone conclusion.

"Um, excuse me," Marrisa interrupted, stepping forward. "I'm not ready yet to allow my daughter to maximize anything until I have a few questions answered."

"But of course you have," Clara smiled, turning the full impact of her gaze onto Marrisa. Again, her eyes glowed with the same strange fire and the effect was immediate. All the tension Marrisa had felt since entering the house quietly drained away, as if someone had open a valve on the bottom of her worry-tank.

Without being aware she did so, Marrisa walked around the other side of the single bed; dreamlike. Reaching out her left hand, Clara laid it gently on Marrisa's left forearm. Clara was still holding onto Priscilla's right forearm and the same display of light and heat in her eyes repeated upon contact with Marrisa.

Marrisa's nostrils flared and her pupils dilated until almost none of the iris was visible. Eyes widened in surprise and shock, Marrisa suddenly burst out in gleeful laughter. Here head snapped from Clara's gaze to Pris' and she immediately began to cry, rivulets of joy coursing down her face while sobs shook her. The scene lasted no more than 15 seconds, but for Pris and her mom it was an eternity. Clara had become a conduit from mother to daughter and both experienced the love, fear, and full avalanche of emotions each elicited in the other.

Recovering, Marissa returned her gaze to Clara; but now her vision was laser sharp. "How can I help?" was all she asked.

Some form of communication was apparently happening between the three as their faces ran the gamut of expressions. Ham had been observing from the doorway and now Frank walked over to him.

"This might take a while," he observed knowingly. "Would you care for something to eat?"

Hamilton had been so enraptured by what was transpiring with Pris that he had barely noticed Frank's approach. Shaking himself, he pivoted his chair around and wordlessly moved down the hallway back toward the front of the house. Frank followed.

SEVEN

"WHAT DID PRIS MEAN when she said you were telekinetic, and how does a roast beef sandwich sound?" Frank asked as they entered the kitchen. As with most homes in America, they didn't eat in the dining room; they ate in the kitchen at a counter which separated it from the dining room.

"Do you have horseradish mayo?" Ham inquired. "I'm glad you said roast beef, as I don't eat ham."

"Oh, Nichols doesn't sound like a Jewish name." Frank replied curiously.

"Not Jewish, just not a cannibal," Ham replied with a grin.

Frank stared at him for a moment before it registered. "That's some defense mechanism you've got there, young man," he observed.

"How's that?" Ham asked.

"Making fun at your own expense, or being self-deprecating. It's a common defense mechanism for someone who either doesn't want people to get too close or who has low self-worth," Frank explained. "I'm fairly certain you have strong self-esteem, so I'm guessing you just don't want to let people in. It's common among adults with disabilities but not so much with teens."

At Ham's look of dubious respect, Frank replied, "I've read a lot in the past ten years while I've helped Clara adjust to her condition. Now she helps me adjust to mine."

"Oh, and what is your condition?" Ham asked as his curiosity was piqued.

"That you eat this sandwich while I make one for myself," Frank deflected in turn, setting a plate holding the quartered sandwich and a handful of cheese puffs in front of Ham at the counter. "I don't know what Priscilla or her mother will want, so I'll wait to ask."

Rather than continuing the sparkling repartee', Ham dove into the meal. As Frank finished making his own and turned from the kitchen counter to sit opposite Ham a soft chime sounded.

Ham looked curiously at Frank, who said, "Clara needs my attention, I'll be right back."

While he was alone Ham took a moment to call his father, who answered on the first ring. "Are you all right?" Martin Nichols asked immediately, concern audible in his voice.

"I'm fine dad, I just haven't had a chance to call until now," Ham replied in his most apologetic voice. "I'm sorry I worried you but things have been just a little crazy. I'm over at Detective Kratos' house and we're all fine."

"Hamilton Nichols, how can you say *things are fine* and *I'm with the police* in the same breath?" Martin asked heatedly. He sounded like he'd been drinking for a while.

"Dad, can I explain it once I get home?" Ham asked hopefully. "It's much too complicated to get into over the phone. Just trust me when I say everything is fine; in fact, everything is great," he concluded on an upbeat note.

"How long before you get home and have you eaten since lunch?" his father asked. "It's nearly seven and you know how you get when you don't eat on schedule."

"Actually I'm eating now," Ham reassured. "Frank made me a sandwich."

"Oh, it's Frank now, is it?" Mr. Nichols replied.

"Dad, can we not do this right now?" Ham pleaded. "There's still a lot going on." When his father got a drunken notion in his head he could be dogmatic about it. "I promise I'm fine. Please don't come over to get me. Mrs. Benson will bring me home. Everything is really good and you'll see that when I'm there. I promise you'll understand it all once I've explained what's been happening."

"When will you be home?" Martin asked again, pointedly.

"I don't know right now," Ham admitted. "But I'm here with Mr. and Mrs. Kratos, Mrs. Benson, and Priscilla. What kind of trouble could I possibly get into?"

EIGHT

"SO YOU'RE THE YOUNG telepath Frank has been telling me about," Clara said. Frank had returned to the kitchen to inform Ham that Clara needed to see him right away.

"Ah, ma'am?" Ham replied, puzzled.

"Did you or did you not force a young man to bludgeon himself with a plastic pitcher after making said young man toss its contents on himself?" Clara asked, grinning.

"Well yes ma'am, I guess I did. But that doesn't make me a telepath; I'm telekinetic according to Pris," Ham replied.

"Well according to *me*, young man, you're both," Clara quipped. "No one can *push* someone to do something against their will without telepathic abilities. And that is the term used in the vernacular. The fact you can also swat people with tree branches does indeed make you telekinetic."

"When you put it that way I sound like a superhero," Ham blushed.

"You are indeed and so is this amazing young lady," Clara agreed while glancing at Pris.

"We've been working through her repertoire of skills and I must say, she's a more powerful *superhero* than I am. I can't decide whether to call myself Clara the Great or Kratos the Magnificent, though they both have a nice ring." Her grin split her face and everyone joined in the good-natured laughter.

"Can I be Hamtastic?" Ham asked as the mirth died down.

"Oh...boo...Ham..." came from three separate mouths simultaneously.

"Seriously, there are powerful and uncertain forces at work in this city and we all must be as prepared as possible if we're going to defeat them," Clara said, breaking the jovial mood. Her eyes were on fire once again and Ham and Frank both noticed it. Frank thought it was a trick of the light but Ham wasn't sure what it was.

"This is beginning to sound like one of my comic books," Ham quipped.

"Yes and there is true evil in the world today, never doubt that," Clara rejoined. "I would prefer more seasoned warriors or at least adults with fully-developed abilities to join with in combat but, *you go to war with the army you have, not the army you wish you had*, to quote Donald Rumsfeld."

"Is it really that immediate?" Frank asked. It was the first time he had spoken since they had all rejoined in Clara's bedroom.

In answer to his question Clara looked at Ham and commanded, "Light that candle." She was pointing at a six-inch pillar setting on a shelf opposite the foot of her bed. When Ham began to turn his chair, Clara's eyes flared white and she barked, "Stop."

Ham looked to her, puzzlement awash on his face; there was definitely something wrong with her eyes. "What?" He asked after receiving no additional directions.

"Do it from here," Clara directed, "with your mind."

"That's not funny," Ham said more sharply than he'd intended.

"Am I laughing?" Clara replied. "Many, in fact most telepathic-telekinetics are also pyrokinetic," she explained. "You just need to believe you can."

"But I don't know how," Ham replied softly.

"You didn't know how to break tree branches but you did," Clara responded. "Concentrate on the candle and think of the wick. Then think of fire and snap your fingers."

Ham made a show of following her directions, turning to face the candle and twisting his face in concentration. Holding his hand out in the same direction he snapped his finger; nothing. Taking a deep breath and settling himself in his chair, he tried again and again; still nothing.

"Well apparently that doesn't work, and I'm okay with it," Ham observed. "Although it would be really cool to be able to start fires with my thoughts."

"Ham, you're not concentrating," Clara chastised. "Your mind was in four other places besides the candle. Your father will be fine, we'll figure out who the Jenkins clones are, Pris loves you already, and no one is going to die tonight. Now concentrate," she barked, her eyes flaring yet again.

Ham's face flamed red at the mention of Pris loving him and Pris glared at Clara as if betrayed. Ham had turned and was also glaring at Clara as he said, "I don't know how you knew I was thinking all that but I don't appreciate my innermost thoughts being shared so publicly. And I can't light a candle just by snapping my damn fingers," he shouted, snapping his fingers to emphasize his rant.

Across the room behind him, the candle leapt to life. Ham didn't see it but he heard the soft whoosh of the ignition, and all other heads in the room had turned to stare at the dancing flame.

"Holy shit!" Ham exclaimed.

"Here, enough of that," Clara remonstrated. "Thou shalt not take my Father's name in vain." Her eyes were aflame and her hair seemed to rise from the sides of her face.

Frank looked searchingly at his wife. "Did you mean to say *Our Father*?" He asked.

Clara sighed in resignation. "It was bound to come out eventually and it may as well be now; Priscilla and Marrisa already know," she replied. "Frank, when I had my first attack from MS it almost killed me," she referenced. "An Archangel of the Lord appeared to me and said I had many great things to accomplish in His name, but I had to be willing to accept *her* into my body in order for *her* power to manifest on Earth."

Pausing, she looked beseechingly at her husband, willing him to accept. "I did, Frank. And now I can speak and think and guide these precious children with *her* help. Her name is Raquel and she is the Archangel of justice and vengeance." Noting the look of utter disbelief on everyone's face, she hurried on. "It is her job to cast demons into Hell and bring peace to our troubled world. We believe these clones, as Ham calls them, are actually demons manifest in human hosts much as I am now."

Frank stared for a long moment before speaking. "How do I know who I'm talking to when you speak if it all sounds the same?"

Clara looked deep into his eyes and replied, "Does it matter as long as we both love you?"

Frank sputtered and stammered, trying to wrap his mind around this immense revelation. "You both love me?"

"Yes, Frank," Raquel replied, and now they all understood why her eyes glowed bright on occasion. "The care and love, compassion and nurturing you've demonstrated in tending to our needs has given me every right to love you."

Frank stepped to the chair beside the bed, holding his hand to his forehead while groping blindly for the chair with the other. His mind was so overwhelmed by the prospect of all he'd just heard that it refused to register anything as mundane as a chair.

"An Archangel of the Lord loves me," was all he was capable of saying.

Everyone else in the room stared in awe at Raquel. She beamed joy and love at them for a moment before speaking. "We have so much work to do and so little time. Ham, light the remainder of the candles in the room; all at once, please."

Ham shook himself like a dog after a bath. Even parts of his body over which he had no control seemed to cooperate in the great awakening caused by this divulgence. Closing his eyes, his face became impassive and every candle in the room ignited.

His eyes sprung open and he breathed the single word, "Yes."

NINE

"WHAT DID YOU MEAN WHEN you said there are demons inhabiting the clones of people?" Pris asked. She had been first to recover from the onslaught of information they had all just received. "Is Mr. Jenkins a clone?"

"If our theory holds true, that's a very real possibility," Raquel replied. "And they can replicate numerous clones of the individual who willingly offers their body for service to Lucifer," she continued. "They're usually made from organic matter and are referred to in Jewish religious history as golems."

"I thought those were made up in the Tolkien stories," Ham replied.

"Really?" Raquel replied. "Did you not know my Father made the original pair of humanity out of clay?" Looking to the ceiling, she spoke to no one in particular. "What are they teaching children these days?"

"So the story of creation is true?" Marrisa interjected.

"That portion of the story is true," Raquel replied. "Much of what mankind has done to the original writings of my Father's prophets is a sad state of affairs. They've taken very simple guidance and twisted it around to fit their narrow-minded, shallow, self-serving need to control everything. Those two were what you today might call Troglodytes and they were around long before modern man. They were created long before the numerous Ice Ages your scientists are fond of talking about."

"Did you say *Ages*, plural?" Frank asked. "How long are we actually talking about?"

"Darling, why on Earth does it matter?" Clara asked through clear blue eyes. "It has no bearing on what we must now focus upon."

"I suppose that's true, but it would be interesting to hear from an actual reliable source regarding how long it's been between creation and now," he replied.

"If I answer your question, can we drop this discussion and get to work on saving the current residents of the planet?" Raquel asked sarcastically, her eyes flaring.

"Ooh, a sarcastic Archangel; I like it," Pris exclaimed.

Raquel looked at her and beamed. "I really enjoy the many subtle nuances of your language," she said. "We don't speak where my Father resides as we're all connected eternally."

Turning to Frank, she added, "Frank, those you refer to as *Adam and Eve* were created by my Father over six million of your years ago. My brothers and sisters and I were remonstrated at that time to always care for and watch over you. The multitude of them who are present this very moment on the planet would stagger your imagination. But we are charged with not interfering in the daily aspects of your lives. We can only intervene when other angelic forces are at play, or if one who is of great importance stands to be injured or killed."

"Are any of us *of great importance*?" Marrisa asked, making air quotes in front of her.

"Unfortunately, I cannot reveal that to anyone about anyone," Raquel replied. "And as I've said much more than I should have," she said, glancing at the ceiling and leaving the sentence unfinished. "We really need to work on how we're going to find out what the Great Deceiver's plans are."

"Can Clara *see* any of them, like when she helped me with cases before?" Frank asked.

"I probably could, but it would be easier if Priscilla did it," Clara replied, back in control.

"If I did *what*?" Pris blurted; dumbfounded. "I can't see where people are."

"You can't *yet*," Clara reminded her. "We have much to train you on and it needs to be done quickly. In the meanwhile it's getting late." Turning to Marrisa, Clara said, "I would ask you to consider allowing Priscilla to come here after school every day for the next week at least."

When Marrisa took a deep breath to object, Clara held a hand up for patience. "I fully understand your reluctance to involve Priscilla in anything dangerous, but we're all so far beyond that." Clara's eyes glowed brightly again, and they could all tell Raquel was back in charge. "If we don't successfully thwart Lucifer's plans before they begin creating their armies, we may not ever be able to stop him."

"I'm sorry what do you mean; armies? And stopping *Lucifer*?" Ham posed. "You make it sound like the end of the world or something."

"My dear, sweet Ham," she replied. "That is exactly what I'm talking about."

TEN

"HOW ARE WE SUPPOSED to find out if one of the Jenkins clones is here or not?" Pris asked Ham under her breath. They were seated in first hour waiting for the tardy bell to ring. Marrisa had taken to dropping Pris off early after she had found out Ham was usually there by seven.

"We can just look around, silly," Ham replied nonchalantly. "This is America, you know. We can look around if we want."

"And if the man with the *gun* decides he might want to keep us quiet he just might shoot us, even in America," Pris countered.

"Yeah, there is that," Ham allowed.

The bell rang and they were headed for their first period. Most of the other students were already in their classrooms as Priscilla had yet to obtain the coveted faster chair. As they rounded the corner in the hall to go to their science class, Butch stepped out in front of them from behind the end of a row of lockers. His usually surly expression was slack this time and he simply stared at them for 20 seconds.

Ham finally had enough and said, "Butch, either do something stupid or get out of the way."

Butch took one step backward without breaking eye contact. He reached toward the wall and put his left hand on the doorknob of the janitor's closet.

"It's a trap," Ham yelled. "Pris, back up, now!"

He commanded his chair forward, heedless the danger which might befall him. Butch grabbed his chair and manhandled it into the closet before quickly closing the door. The closet was narrow enough Ham couldn't turn his chair around and it was dark. Groping for the light switch he figured must be next to the doorknob, his fingers brushed the cover plate. As he reached again, someone grabbed him from in front and clamped a hand over his mouth and nose.

Instantly his right hand closed into a fist and he lashed out at whoever was holding him, with unexpected results. Whoever was holding him had not anticipated being punched by a thirteen-year-old boy in a wheelchair. They had especially not been expecting this boy to be telekinetic. When his fist made contact there was a momentary resistance like punching a pillow; then there was nothing. The hand covering his mouth and nose was gone.

Gasping for breath he punched the air over his head in a backward motion, thinking about the door bursting open; and it did. The knob rebounded off the locker next to the closet and Ham was rolling backward into the hall. Glancing around he spotted Priscilla being pushed down the hall toward the rear exit by a man and a woman, neither of whom he had ever seen.

"Hey, stop," he yelled as he turned his chair and gave pursuit.

The woman looked back before redoubling her effort to push the chair faster. Now Priscilla's slow chair was to her benefit. The gearing could be disengaged for pushing if one knew how, but apparently these two did not. The gear drive in her chair complained loudly as the pair tried to move it faster toward the exit. Ham was gaining on them and was frantic with fear. *What were they going to do with Pris?* he thought in almost blind panic.

"Help," he screamed at the top of his lungs. "Help me."

And then he remembered what the police officer in the seventh grade had told him if there was ever anyone trying to abduct or harm him; yell fire.

"Fire," he screamed, "Fire, fire, fire," he repeated. A separate part of his mind told him he sounded like a captain in charge of a firing squad, but he ignored it.

Closing to within ten feet of where the couple had the door open, Ham could see a dark green service van outside with a driver. Another large, muscular man was standing beside the open sliding door. Still yelling, Ham released his hold on the joystick of his chair and thrust his clenched fist in the direction of the closest man's back. Even though he was still eight feet away, the effect was immediate.

The man struggling with Priscilla's chair arched his back as if he'd been punched in the kidney. Grunting in pain, he grabbed his lower back with both hands. The woman whirled on Ham, flying at his face. Her hands were extended with her fingers hooked into claws, and a harsh growl emanated from deep in her throat.

Ham punched at her hands as he caught a glimpse of the man outside lunging for the door. When his fist contacted her wrist, the woman vanished. The man outside skidded to a halt, eyes as large as the orbits would allow. Spinning, he leapt and dove into the open van door screaming, "Go, go!"

The driver spun the tires as he floored the gas pedal and the van hesitated for a moment, seeking traction. The man inside had seen his partner vanish and suddenly his aching back was of little importance. He charged through the double-glass doors, striking the right one hard enough to crack the tempered glass.

In three leaping strides he dove into the van just as it rocketed away down the service lane behind the school. It didn't slow as it reached the street but slewed left as the driver cranked the wheel over, trying to turn into the thoroughfare. The two inside tires left the pavement and the large, top-heavy vehicle precariously wobbled down the road for 30 feet on two wheels. Righting itself it fell back onto all four tires, swaying from side-to-side as it sped away.

Ham was immediately at Pris' side calling her name. "Pris, are you okay? Did they hurt you? Look at me. Say something, Pris," he rapid-fired questions and demands.

"If you'll shut up for a second, I will," she replied, laughing.

"What could possibly be funny about this?" he bellowed.

"You saved me," she smiled. "You really saved me," she said again. "And did you make that woman disappear?"

The question brought them both up short. Students were piling into the hallways and Ham worried one or more of them had witnessed the woman vanishing. That would be really hard to explain. But all the students and teachers had apparently seen was the man charging out the door and the van careening away. One older male student had run out the door behind it. He came back in now using his cell phone.

"This is Adam Banicker, I'm a senior at Chickasha West," he said. "I'm a Citizen's Corp VIPS cadet and I just witnessed an attempted kidnapping. I have a vehicle description and partial license plate." Adam continued to walk toward the front of the school and the rest was unclear. Pris recognized him as the tall young man who had held the door for her the first day of class.

Pris looked at Ham with unfettered adoration in her eyes, immediately embarrassing him. "Aw come on, Pris. Make a snide remark, be mean if you have to, but don't look at me like that. I don't know how to respond," he groused.

She only laughed out loud before directing her chair as close to him as possible. Speaking softly, she said, "You'll just have to get used to it, bucko. If I could kiss you I would." Blowing softly on the tube, she turned her chair toward the front of the school. "We need to talk to Frank, right now," she called over her shoulder.

ELEVEN

"WHERE DO YOU SUPPOSE they went?" Frank asked finally.

They had been trying to recount the story in Clara's bedroom for the better part of an hour. They would make it through about 10 minutes of recalling the event before one of the three adults would stop them. Whether it was to clarify a point or express amazement at the brazenness of the would-be abductors, Ham and Pris were both running out of patience. Ham had just retold the scene where the woman had disappeared.

"I don't know and I really don't care," he replied.

"And I'm not saying you did anything wrong Ham, but I am concerned they might turn up again," Frank explained. "If your teleportation was…unpleasant for them, they might come back with a vengeance."

Clara had quietly listened for most of the tale but now addressed Ham. "The possibility exists you may have sent them to another dimension, another planet, or absolutely nowhere; into the void. I know so very little about it."

"What?" Ham burst out. "You mean I might have killed them? Does Raquel know?"

Clara shook her head. "If she does she's not saying. Wait; she says we shall know when we must."

"What is that supposed to mean?" Frank asked.

Clara shrugged. "She can be very disingenuous when she wants." She looked at Pris. "If I help you understand how to see someone perhaps you can find them, if they're still in this plane. Your connection to Ham will facilitate it."

Pris looked doubtful but rolled over next to Clara's bedside. When Clara touched her arm it was clear from the brightness in her eyes that Raquel was also involved. Marrisa was still uncertain about this whole training thing but after all, Raquel was an Archangel; what could possibly go wrong? Archangels were supposed to be the epitome of faith and trust; weren't they?

Pris' hair lifted from around her ears and her face went slack. Marrisa was about to say something when Clara released her arm. Pris turned her chair to face the rest and her eyes appeared to have some of the same residual glow in them, but it faded quickly.

"I can see the woman, probably because she was next to me, but I can't see the man from the closet at all," she informed them.

"That actually makes sense," Frank said. "When Clara helps me locate someone I have to give her their picture or something they had close to them recently. You saw the woman but not the man."

"Where is the woman?" Ham asked fretfully. He had been inconsolable after Clara had explained he might have sent them to another dimension, or another planet.

"Lake Tahoe," Pris said.

"Huh? Do what?" Ham replied.

"She was seen swimming fully clothed in Lake Tahoe," Pris clarified.

"How do you know that?" Marissa asked.

"When I thought about her after Clara or Raquel showed me how, I saw her fall into a lake," Pris explained. "She fell from about 20 feet I'd say, and came up spluttering. She immediately started swimming toward the nearest shore and when she got out, there was a sign which read *Welcome to Lake Tahoe.*"

"So she's alive?" Ham enthused.

"Yep, and mad as a wet hen," Pris chortled.

Everyone grinned. "Well then, I guess we can assume the man got sent somewhere on earth as well," Frank said, sounding as equally relieved.

"There is a way to test it," Marrisa offered.

"No!" Pris exclaimed.

"You haven't even heard what I was going to suggest," Marrisa said curiously.

"Yes I did and no, Ham is not going to send you anywhere," Pris said with cold finality.

"So you can read my mind now?" Marrisa asked hesitantly.

"Not so much read as hear ideas, and only ones which elicit strong emotions," Pris responded. "And Ham is of the same opinion."

"Wait, how...oh never mind; strong emotion," he said lamely. "So I guess I have to start guarding my thoughts now," he finished morosely.

"You can never guard that part from me Ham, and I don't have to be a mind-reader to know it," Pris said, grinning widely.

Ham flamed crimson, and closed his eyes in the eternal gesture of the all-suffering male in the presence of an argument he can't win with a female. Clara and Marrisa laughed while Frank walked over to pat him on the shoulder.

"Welcome to adult relationships," he said. "I'm sure you'll do as well as Clara and I have. Let's have some dinner and we'll talk more about who I think these people are that tried to grab you. How's Chinese?"

AFTER FRANK AND MARRISA had cleared away the take-out containers and fortune cookie wrappers they settled in on the sofa and chair in the living room. Clara had insisted on being the hostess and Frank had obligingly placed her in the motor chair kept in her bedroom closet. She could use both arms, although the left one had little strength, and she had a joystick similar to Ham's for guidance.

"The van was stolen and has been recovered. We pulled several recent prints off the interior and one came back as a twice-convicted felon. He was probably the big guy you saw outside," Frank said looking at Ham, who nodded.

"The prints off Pris' chair and the door at the school have yet to yield any results but we'll keep them on file. Everyone on the detective force is working to connect the dots on known associates from the one we have," he informed them. "And there's a BOLO out on him. Now it's just a matter of grunt-work and luck to find the others."

"We still haven't addressed the question of why they tried," Marrisa reminded him. It had been her first question but Frank had asked her to hold off on that until he had a better picture of the day's events.

"I'm sure it has something to do with Pris and Ham's abilities," Clara said suddenly.

And just like that, the pieces fell into place. Any doubt as to their abilities or the importance of their mission was set aside. Marrisa was nodding vigorously and Frank had a deadly serious expression on his face. Pris and Ham looked worried but one look at Clara, whose eyes were blazing bright, led them to know they had extra protection should they need it.

"Ham and Pris shouldn't go back to school until these people are arrested," Frank said.

"They can't miss that much school," Marrisa countered.

"It would be even more embarrassing for us to go around campus with a police escort," Pris added.

"I have to work," Marrisa said. "Who will look after them if they're not in school? I still say they need to be in school. What chance is there they'll even try again, now that they know Ham's abilities?"

"That may be all the more reason for them to try again," Frank responded. "And there's nothing saying they won't try it in the school parking lot or anywhere on campus. Professional snatch and grab artists will use any means necessary to accomplish their goal; be it tranquilizer darts, a club to the head, or whatever."

"And Ham isn't their target," he persisted. "Pris is. He just happened to be in the way, so I can't risk they'll try to take him out of play." He paused for dramatic effect. "And yes that means exactly what you think it means."

They discussed and argued and discussed some more. It was finally agreed that Pris and Ham would spend their days training with Clara and Raquel. Marrisa would bring Pris by in the morning and collect her in the evening.

Frank would pick Ham up in the morning and take him home in the evening once Mr. Nichols was home. All transportation of the two teens would have a police escort. All three residences would have a patrol car with two officers outside at all times and Frank would be inside except for the times he was transporting or running errands. They felt like they had everything covered.

TWELVE

"MOM, CHECK THIS OUT," Pris announced as Marrisa walked through the front door of the Kratos house.

As her mother turned to observe, Pris turned her chair toward the flat screen TV hanging on the wall at the foot of Clara's bed and closed her eyes. The screen flared for a moment before watery images of a woman swimming in a large body of water became visible. The woman was fully clothed and swam to the nearby shore, where she strode out of the water past a sign which read "Welcome to Lake Tahoe."

"What is that?" Marrisa asked, staggered. "Is that the woman who tried to kidnap you?"

"Yes, and Frank has been able to record it and take it to his IT people who have sharpened the image enough to make a positive ID on her," Pris beamed proudly.

"How did you explain coming up with the recording?" Marrisa asked Frank heatedly.

"Do what?" Pris cried. "Not *how did you do that?* Or even *that's absolutely amazing, Priscilla,* just *how did he explain having it?*" Pris was evidently hurt. She had expected her mother to effuse over this newfound skill.

"I'm very impressed, in fact, I'm dumbfounded," Marrisa replied. "But I'm more concerned with how Frank explained to his department the origin of the recording, being as he's a *reasonable and logical man.*" She rounded on him. "How could you possible endanger my daughter by prompting questions you obviously couldn't answer?"

Frank's face was a mask of impassivity. He waited for Marrisa to wind down before he spoke softly. "I explained that a contact I have in Tahoe had seen the posting from a local fisherman who had taken a video of a woman swimming in the lake. It was significant because it happened in the fall when the water is pretty darn cold, and the woman was fully clothed. I further explained how he had found it on a chat site about odd things people do in Tahoe."

Holding up his hand, he continued as Marrisa deflated. "I have a lot of contacts across the western states because I'm known as the detective who deals with odd, unusual, and even paranormal sightings."

Marrisa stood with her face downcast for a long while before Frank approached her and touched her arm. "Do you honestly think I would do anything to jeopardize these children? I love them as if they were my own."

Marrisa pulled away from his hand and walked to where Pris sat, still glaring at her. Kneeling in front of her daughter's chair, she reached and took one of Priscilla's hands. "I'm sorry I overreacted. I've been worried sick since the kidnapping attempt. I just wish we could all go somewhere that no one could find us until this all goes away."

Shaking her head before anyone could retort, she continued. "I know that's not possible as I truly believe there is more at stake here than most people could even imagine. But it doesn't stop me from wishing it."

Rising, she walked back over to Frank. "I apologize for thinking less of you than I should," she offered.

Tears were brimming on the verge of her lower eyelids and she squeezed them away with a pinch of her thumb and forefingers. Frank reached out and gathered her into his arms, holding her quietly as she cried into his shoulder. After she recovered they all shared their thoughts on how they could possibly capitalize on Pris' newfound ability.

"Have you tried any other electronics, like an LCD display on an appliance or a computer screen?" Marrisa asked.

"No, we just discovered it late this morning," Clara replied. "Frank actually sent it to his IT person on that computer in the corner," she said, pointing at a small laptop. Priscilla was already facing the computer and focusing on it. The screen bloomed and settled into the same display they had seen before.

"Try thinking about someone you know," Frank recommended.

"I really don't know anyone that well," Pris replied. "And I'm certainly not in complete control of this ability yet."

"How about Butch?" Marrisa suggested. "Isn't he the one you said shoved Ham into a closet?"

"I really don't like thinking about him," Pris replied.

"This isn't about like or dislike, it's about pushing your talent," Raquel reminded her sternly, causing Clara's eyes to flare.

Turning back to the flat screen TV, Pris closed her eyes. Instantly the screen blossomed and they could all see Ham sitting in a room, staring out the window. As they watched, he wheeled backward from whatever it was he saw, recoiling in fear.

"I thought you were thinking about Butch?" Frank asked.

"I am, but this is what I see," Pris replied, confusion apparent in her voice and face.

The door of the room burst open and they could see a sidewalk and grass with a street further away. Three men rushed into the room and Ham punched at one as soon as he cleared the threshold. The lead man flew backward, taking the second one with him back out the door.

The third man had dropped to a prone position and now extended a pistol in Ham's direction. Before Ham could change his focus and draw his arm back, a dart appeared sticking out of his chest. He raised a shaking hand toward it as he slumped forward against the restraints of his wheelchair.

Priscilla screamed and fainted.

Frank was immediately on the radio to the unit outside Ham's home; they had seen the front bumper of it through the open door. Even as Ham collapsed, Pris' vision had turned back to the door and they had watched the man on the floor disappear. Two other bodies sprawled unmoving on the sidewalk. The patrol officers did not respond.

THIRTEEN

"MR. NICHOLS HAD GONE to the store for some groceries and had only planned to be gone an hour. The officers knew Ham was alone and one offered to remain inside with him, but Ham said he was fine," Frank explained. His face was haggard and he drew a ragged breath before continuing.

"Both officers are in the hospital expected to make a full recovery. One had been shot with the same or a similar dart pistol; the other had been punched in the head and knocked unconscious through his open car window," he finished.

"That must have been some punch," Marrisa commented.

"You're telling me," Frank replied. "The ER doctor said he has torn muscles in his neck like he'd been in a car wreck." He continued, "In fact, the doc said it could have broken his neck."

"What kind of a person can punch hard enough to break a person's neck?" Marrisa asked, startled.

"Oh it's very possible to do so," Frank confirmed. "It only takes 64 pounds of pressure to snap the neck. I've seen training videos of men hopped-up on PCP and other hallucinogens who could punch through a solid wooden door. The explanation on that video stated the pressure required to do *that* is in excess of 200 pounds." They all sat mute for several minutes, astonished by this revelation.

Pris finally broke the silence. "Does anyone know if Ham is alright?"

"They took him to the ER with the officers and he's coming around by last report. Apparently the kidnappers wanted to make sure they put him out quickly so they gave him a very heavy dose," Frank said, shaking his head. "The two he *punched* have yet to awaken. They appear to be in some sort of unusual coma."

"I wish I could go see him, I feel so helpless," Pris said morosely.

"Behold, I have set before you an open door, which no one is able to shut. I know that you have but little power, and yet you have kept my word and have not

denied my name," Clara said monotonously while staring straight ahead; trance-like.

"What did you say?" Marrisa asked, moving alongside Clara's bed. Clara's eyes were open but unseeing.

"Be faithful unto death, and I will give you the crown of life," she said again in the vacant monotone she had used the first time.

"She's quoting Revelation," Frank said. "The first one is about your power I think, and a reminder that you have it. The second one I'm not so sure about."

"Try to see Ham," Marrisa said in a rush.

"Oh of course," Pris exclaimed. "I'm sitting here feeling sorry for myself instead of using God's gift. But there's no TV out here."

They were in the kitchen, having gone in to eat an early dinner. Frank had placed Clara in her chair because she had little company and wanted to take full advantage of it when she did. She was positioned at one end of the counter and Pris was at the other.

"We only have one in the bedroom because I only watch it with Clara," Frank said, looking worriedly at his wife. She still stared vacantly into the middle distance but her breathing was slow and regular.

"Try using the mirror on the wall next to the hallway," Marrisa suggested.

"Huh?" Pris said, confusion dancing across her features. "Mom, the mirror isn't plugged in and isn't used to communicate." She spoke as if she were explaining something to a young child having difficulty grasping a concept.

"Young lady, you may not use that tone of voice with me," Marrisa replied harshly. "I saw a movie once where a magician used a mirror to talk to people in another country," she explained stiffly, as if embarrassed.

"Hey, can't hurt to try," Frank admonished. "You said yourself; you have no idea the limits of what you can do."

Dutifully yet hesitant, Pris turned to face the mirror which was about 20 feet away. Closing her eyes she sighed as she relaxed, thinking about Ham. "Mirror, mirror, on the wall..." she began.

The reflection of the room they were in, as seen from several different angles, shimmered for a moment before it disappeared. In its place was a sharp, crisp image of Ham in a hospital bed. An IV ran into his left arm and his right lay across his chest. As they watched, a woman came in and consulted his chart before glancing around the room. She stealthily pulled a syringe from her smock pocket and moved toward the IV bag. Frank was immediately on his radio.

"Get in Ham's room now," he screamed into the microphone. "There's a woman I don't think belongs in there and she's about to inject something into him or his IV."

As they continued to watch the drama unfold, an officer burst through the door, weapon drawn. There was no sound, but you could tell by the way she flinched he had shouted at her. She held up her hands, assurance and calm radiating from her as her lips moved and she gestured toward Ham's unconscious form.

The officer wasn't hearing it. He'd been ordered to stop her and that was his intent. Shrugging, the woman began to pocket the syringe while walking toward the officer. As he backed toward the door he spoke something to her again, and this time she lunged at him as she pulled the syringe from her pocket.

It was apparent she intended to inject the officer with the contents and as her hand began the downward arc toward his chest, the pistol in his erupted. The concussion from the discharge was obvious in the way the air between them rippled and the woman staggered backward, grasping her abdomen.

Realizing she was found out she turned the syringe on herself and jabbed it into her own neck while thumbing the plunger down. She convulsed once before dropping to her knees. As she fell forward onto her face she threw her arms out to her sides as her legs and back locked in a rigid spasm. The officer could be seen shouting into his shoulder mic and the sound of his voice came out of Frank's radio.

"Officer needs assistance, room 113, recovery ward." Then the mirror was just a mirror.

"What is going on?" Pris nearly screamed the words. "That woman just tried to kill Ham."

Frank was busy on the radio, shouting orders. "Nobody moves her body until I get there, is that understood? Double the guards; one outside the door and one in the room on the other side of the bed. Inside officer to stay as far away from the door as possible and everyone remain extra vigilant. Clear the floor of all non-essential personnel. Acknowledge." He was headed for the front door, still talking on the hand-held.

"Jennings, Omikawa, get inside here now. I want two more cars here immediately; one in front and one on the next block watching the back of this house. Move," he barked.

Frank yanked the front door open without waiting for a response from the officers outside. Clara screamed his name as a blast came through the opening doorway, accompanied by a brilliant fireball of light.

FOURTEEN

AS FRANK WAS BLOWN back into the room, four men rushed through the open doorway. Dust filled the air and the blast had caused all three women's ears to begin ringing painfully. Marrisa had risen from her chair to walk toward the front door, intent on asking Frank what he was going to do about them if he left. She had stopped when she heard him calling the officers in from outside.

Now she was thrown backward, landing flat and knocking the air from her lungs with an explosive grunt Pris heard and felt even over the explosion. She tried to call for her mom but her voice wasn't working. In fact, nothing was working. She was struggling just to draw a breath.

Clara was slumped in her chair, her eyes closed.

"Grab the girl," she heard someone yell as if from a great distance.

"What about the other two?" called a different voice.

"Leave them, it's the girl he wants," the first voice said.

One of the men began fumbling with her chair motor, trying to disengage the drive coupling so the chair could be pushed. As he finished this the third man grabbed the chair from behind and whirled it toward the door; inconsiderate of Priscilla's body being slammed around in the chair's confines.

"Stop," Pris tried to shout. It was all she could do, and poorly. She repeatedly tried with every fiber of her being until it was a full-throated scream.

"Shut up or I'll stuff a towel in your mouth," the man growled in her ear. Pris just kept screaming.

As they reached the door two more men appeared just outside. All six were carrying tactical rifles at the ready except her driver; his was slung across his back. Abruptly Marrisa leapt to her feet and dashed toward the group. One of the men at the door was facing in and saw her coming. Shouting a warning he turned the barrel of his rifle toward her and brought it to his shoulder.

Throwing her hand out in front of her, palm out and fingers splayed upward, Marrisa shouted something unintelligible. A crashing boom of noise, light, and force struck the two men in the doorway, flinging them out into the night. Two of the original four men whirled to face her, bringing their weapons to bear, and were greeted with a repeat of her previous display.

One was hurled against the wall next to the door with sufficient force to break through the sheetrock. The other attacker slammed into the open door, knocking it off its hinges while he crashed into the wall before rebounding onto the floor. The door fell heavily onto his still form.

The other man who had disengaged the chair's drive was close enough he could reach out and touch Marrisa and he did so; or at least, he tried. As he lunged for her she slashed the same outthrust hand across the air in front of his face and he spun into the center of the room.

The man would have made Baryshnikov jealous the way he was pirouetting across the carpet. He spun five or six times before his upper body weight pulled him down. Hitting the floor, he bounced into the far wall where he remained motionless.

The remaining man shoved the wheelchair toward the open door and whirled, his hand outstretched in a similar manner as Marrisa. An azure ball of energy appeared between the two, writhing and roiling around like a huge display of St. Elmo's Fire. Red streamers crackled and spit out of the ball and it shifted back and forth between the two for several seconds and the air reeked of ozone.

"*Commendare*," Marrisa shouted, bringing her second hand into position alongside her first.

As the ball moved decidedly toward the man he mimicked her pose and arrested its movement. Now it remained between them, closer to the man than before but still roiling and sizzling.

"*Imperium commendare*," Marrisa screamed, and the ball began moving toward the man again.

He slid backward across the carpeted floor, his hiking boots making tearing noises as they sought traction in the fibers. Her opponent continued his backward struggle into the corner by the doorway and now had nowhere else to go. Fear danced across his face, followed by determination. Hunching his shoulders and screaming a hoarse war cry, he redoubled his effort.

But the ball kept moving toward him until it touched his outstretched fingertips. There was a blinding flash like looking at an arc welder when it makes contact, only much larger. It was followed immediately by a concussion which seemed to shake the very foundation of the house; the man vaporized.

He didn't disappear. The action happened very quickly, but slowly enough for Pris to see. Her chair had rolled to a stop near the front door facing into the same corner in which the battle had culminated. The man simply...dissolved.

Pris tried to turn her chair to face her mother, intent on demanding to know just what in the Blue Hades was going on but the drive was still disengaged. She could just turn her head far enough to see her mother's eyes roll back before she collapsed onto the carpet.

Pris called into the night sky for several minutes before one of the police officers on duty outside staggered up the walk in response. His face was a bloody mask and he was dragging his left leg. His right arm dangled uselessly at his side, but he was trying to reach his epaulet mic with his left hand.

"Officers down. Officer needs assistance, Lieutenant Kratos' house. The LT is down. I repeat, the LT is down. Three suspects also down. Officer needs assistance right now, damnit!" he finished.

Pris looked at the tattered man and hesitated to ask him if he could reengage her drive. She knew she needed to at least be out of the way for the ensuing chaos.

"Sir, I hate to bother you at a time like this but can I tell you how to engage the drive on my chair so I can get out of the way, please?" she asked as calmly as she could manage.

She could see his name badge on his shirt: Omikawa. The officer stared at her blankly as if he couldn't comprehend the request.

"Officer Omikawa, can you help me please?" Pris tried again. Omikawa shook himself, grimacing in pain. His face flushed and Pris thought for a moment he might pass out.

Then his eyes cleared and focused. He looked at her carefully and said, "Tell me what to do."

THE HOUSE WAS INDEED chaos; at least a dozen police officers and plainclothes detectives crowded into the living room. Frank had been rushed away via ambulance; Pris heard someone say *critical condition*. Clara was coming back around and two policemen had picked the limp form of Marrisa Benson off the floor. She was still unconscious and, after first assessing her vitals, they laid her gently on the sofa.

Officer Omikawa had at first refused to be treated until Frank and the women were seen to but he'd been outvoted by the paramedics. They'd taken one look at him and immediately forced him to the floor. He now sat in the kitchen at the counter, an untouched cup of coffee cooling in front of him.

He'd repeated the story to investigators at least three times and was tired of talking. His head was bandaged and his right arm was in a sling and swath. He'd lost one of his shoes somewhere along the way and his stocking foot rested on the ring of the stool. Pris sat next to him, sipping water from a bottle with a straw someone had found in a drawer in the kitchen.

"You really should go home and get some rest," Pris told him. He did indeed look like he was ready to pass out.

"I'm not sure I can make it that far," he replied. "I surely can't drive and I don't want to take another officer away from the investigation just to chauffeur me home."

"Why don't you go down the hall and lay down in Frank's bedroom?" Pris suggested. "I'm pretty sure he won't be home tonight." And then she had burst out crying in great, jagged sobs which wracked her body.

"Hey, hey, it's over now; everyone will be okay," he soothed.

"How can you say that?" she wailed. "Frank is in critical condition, my mom is unconscious and Clara seems to be stuck somewhere in la-la land."

"Actually, I'm just back from la-la land and it was NOT a pleasant journey," Clara said from the other end of the counter.

"Oh, my goodness, I'm so glad to hear your voice," Pris enthused.

"And I yours, young lady," Clara replied. "Tell me what happened."

Looking directly at her, Pris locked her eyes with Clara's before cutting them toward Omikawa. "I'm not really sure where to begin," she fudged.

"Officer, this is my home," Clara informed him. "I would be pleased if you would do as this young lady suggested. Go down the hall to the second door on the right and lie down on the bed. You can remove your soiled shirt if you desire or just stretch out on top of the blanket. I really don't mind either way." Clara's eyes had glowed as she spoke and now Omikawa rose from his stool.

"Thank you, ma'am. I believe I'll do just that," he said, now under Raquel's influence. He stood and stumbled toward the hall.

"Now tell me," Clara said urgently.

When she told Clara about Frank the woman seemed to age right before her eyes. She sighed deeply then focused on Pris again. "Continue." After recounting the battle between her mother and the attacker, Clara's eyes glowed fiercely. "Are you sure she said *Imperium Commendare*, child? Be absolutely certain."

"Yes I'm certain. Where else would I have even heard such words?" Pris asked belligerently. "What do they mean anyway?"

"They're words of power only angels can use," Raquel replied. "And only certain angels; warrior angels." She paused to consider. "It would appear one of my brethren interceded on our behalf while I was indisposed. He must have taken control of your mother's body as she was the only person here capable of unrestricted movement."

She paused, considering the importance of the action. "It was a serious breach of protocol and a price will be paid. But the fact that one of the attackers could respond to her in kind means only one thing; at least a second hierarchy demon was in possession of that body. It is the only way one of our own would be allowed to interfere."

"What is a second hierarchy demon?" Pris asked, enthralled and aghast simultaneously.

"There will be time for me to share all of our history with you," Raquel said. "But right now we need to get to the hospital and see to Frank and Ham. Things are advancing much more rapidly than I had feared."

"Who can take us?" Pris observed. "I don't think any of these policemen will, and mom's still out."

"Actually mom's right here," Marrisa said from the entrance to the living room.

"Mom," Pris shouted. Heads turned her way but she didn't even care.

"Oh baby girl, I'm so sorry you had to go through all this," Marrisa said as she moved to embrace her daughter.

"Mom, did you know you were inhabited by an angel; a warrior angel?" Pris whispered.

Marrisa's head whipped around to Clara, her eyes locking on like a radar tracking system in a fighter plane. "Is that so?" she observed casually.

"Marrisa, there is much to discuss and even more to explain, but for right now we need to get to the hospital," Raquel said pointedly. "As one of my brethren was so bold as to enter your body unbidden, Frank and Ham must be in grievous danger."

Marrisa looked at her long and hard. "I'll get the van warmed up," she said.

"There's no time," Raquel replied. "We must make all haste to get to them. I fear the worst."

"Well then let's go," Marrisa said.

She grabbed her purse and headed toward the garage, then had a second thought. Returning to the kitchen counter, she picked up Omikawa's radio from where he had left it. Glancing around, she slipped it in her purse.

FIFTEEN

"I'M CLARA KRATOS. MY husband, Detective Lieutenant Frank Kratos, was brought here recently by ambulance," Clara explained to the ER nurse. "I need to see him right away. It involves the case and is a matter of extreme importance."

"I'm sorry Mrs. Kratos, but your husband is in surgery," the nurse replied. "You'll have to wait for the surgeon or one of the team to come out in order to find out any information. As far as speaking to him, that's just not possible right now."

"Where can we wait that one of the team may find us?" Clara asked calmly.

"I can lead you to the ICU waiting room but it's for immediate family only," she said, eyeing the others.

"This is Frank's sister Marrisa and her daughter Priscilla. They've been staying with us," she lied easily.

"Very well ma'am, if you'll follow me?"

Nothing was said about the deception Clara had used on the ER nurse. It was more expedient than trying to explain all the reasons why they were together. Once in the ICU waiting room she turned toward Marrisa.

"Do you think you can find out where Hamilton is?" Clara asked in a stage whisper.

"Probably, it's not a very big hospital," Marrisa replied. Why do you want to know?"

"There are some wards Raquel can place on his room to keep anyone associated with the demonic bunch from entering but she has to be physically in the room," Clara explained.

"I'm sure there will be several guards posted as well as who-knows-what else after Frank was injured," Marrisa reminded her. "And do we even know what exactly happened to Frank? Was he shot?"

"There was an explosion at the door just as he opened it and he flew backward into the room," Pris explained.

She had told her part of the story to at least three officers or detectives and Clara, but now realized her mother had not been privy to any of those conversations. She hit the high points again so as not to delay the quest for Ham.

"When I get back or when there's a dull moment, you *will* explain to me how a Warrior Angel can just take over my body, right?" Marrisa asked pointedly of Clara.

Eyes flashing, Raquel spoke. "In days past some considered it a rare honor to be the vessel for any angel, especially one of the warrior caste," she stated rather aloofly.

"And given the choice I would be honored to do the same," Marrisa said to mollify the angel. "I just want to hear how it can be done without my permission."

"And so you shall, at the very next *dull moment* we have," Raquel assured her.

Marrisa went off down the hallway toward the main lobby, ostensibly to find a directory to inform her of where Ham might be. Pris turned her gaze on Raquel to ask other clarifying questions about the recent events only to find Clara gazing once again at nothing.

"Clara?" she asked. There was no reply.

IN THE MAIN LOBBY, which was closed now after hours, lights were dimmed and the only person in sight was a custodian running a floor buffer. Walking to the directory marquee, she ran a finger down the list of departments until she found the general in-patient ward. It was on the second floor in the other wing of the building. Turning to look for the elevator she noticed the custodian watching her leave.

Looking back she was shocked to see his eyes glowing a bright golden hue. Hurriedly punching the call button, she prayed for the elevator to arrive before he made a move toward her. She was afraid he was a demon. When it arrived the janitor turned his back to her.

Backing into the car she glanced over to locate and press the button for the second floor. She had looked away for no more than two seconds but when she looked back into the lobby, the janitor was nowhere in sight. She shifted nervously until the elevator doors closed without incident.

When she stepped off the elevator she was in radiology and it was closed. A sign on the wall pointed her to the in-patient ward and she moved in that direction. Coming to a set of closed double-doors with no knob or pull handle she could see down the long hallway to where a policeman was standing watch outside a room. Nurses and other staff bustled about on the floor and she watched for several minutes, trying to judge her best way of getting them all into Ham's room. The elevator behind her dinged.

Freezing, she glanced around quickly but she saw no place to hide and nothing to use as an impromptu weapon. Deciding instead to go with the *lost, looking for the bathroom* routine she turned to see who else was getting off in radiology after hours. The custodian from the lobby stepped off and strode unthreateningly toward her.

"I'm a little lost," she said with a self-deprecating laugh. "I was looking for the ladies room and..."

His eyes flashed gold momentarily, and he smiled disarmingly as he spoke softly. "I respect your desire to stay out of trouble but that is the second-most lame excuse anyone uses for being where they aren't supposed to be."

"And what's the first?" Marrisa grinned. "God, I hope you're an angel; otherwise I'm in deep doo-doo."

"I do so love all the colloquialisms of your language," he said, chuckling silently. "I can help you get into Hamilton's room but I doubt seriously the rest of you can join in," he said, still smiling.

"How...okay, time to do some *'splainin' Lucy*," she said, the smile on her face being replaced by a frown of uncertainty.

"My name is Uriel and Raquel is my sister," he said. "It was I who inhabited your body recently, a fact of which I am sorely remorseful. There was no alternative if I was to protect the anointed one and my sister at the same time."

"Wait, wait," Marrisa stammered. "You inhabited my body and fought off the bad guys including, apparently, a second-hierarchy demon?"

Looking startled, Uriel lowered his eyes briefly, before looking back into hers. "Indeed it was a first-hierarchy demon, Berith to be exact. He was a prince of the Cherubim before the great battle."

"So you killed him, using my body?" Marrisa said, aghast.

"No, it is almost impossible to *kill* any of my brothers and sisters, regardless whether they reside with my Father or...elsewhere," he explained. "All I did was to destroy the vessel which Berith inhabited."

Shaking herself, Marrisa recalled her mission. "There's plenty of time I hope, to ask all the questions I have but right now I need to get Raquel into that room," she said, pointing down the hall. "She needs to ward it against demons? Did I say that right?"

"Indeed, you said it exactly right," Uriel replied. "And I can help you there. I can walk these halls freely in this vessel thanks to the good man who actually is the custodian. Say hello, Carl."

The fire in Uriel's eyes vanished and a pair of soft brown ones regarded her humbly.

"So, we gets ta be Archangel vessels, huh?" he asked, grinning. "Sumpin' ta tell muh grankids 'bout, cep'in I ain't got none, and dey wouldn't b'lieve me anywho."

"Well Carl, there was a little difference for you and I; my use wasn't consensual," Marrisa said, blushing when she thought how she made it sound like they had been intimate.

"Nutin' much mo' inimate dan havin' a angel inside ya, huh?" Carl replied, reading her face.

Grinning, Marrisa extended her hand in the time-honored gesture of friendship. "Nice to meet you Carl but Uriel and I have places to go."

Shaking her hand, Carl said, "My pleasure, ma'am," and then his eyes flared golden again. "Follow me," Uriel said.

Taking a pass card from his breast pocket, he swiped the sensor on the wall and the red light turned green. There was a soft click and the right-hand door snicked open about two inches. Slipping his fingers into the crack of the handle-less door Uriel pulled it open and stood aside; allowing Marrisa to enter first. They walked abreast up the hallway to Ham's room and stopped in front of the officer.

"There's a mess in there I need to clean up and this is my helper," he said to the officer. His eyes flared brightly and a warm, welcoming smile sprang onto the officer's face as if he had just recognized a favorite long-lost relative.

"Certainly Carl, go right on in," he replied readily. "You too miss."

As soon as they entered Ham was on high alert, as was the officer seated on the other side of the bed.

"Sorry, you can't be in here," the officer said. "And what happened to Phil?" he finished, reaching for his sidearm and radio simultaneously.

"Its fine Daniel," Uriel said, holding out his hand placatingly. His eyes glowed a mellow gold and the other officer relaxed noticeably.

"Oh, well alright," Daniel said. "I'll just wait out in the hall."

When the door closed Ham looked from Marrisa to Uriel and back. "Are you okay or are you being held hostage by this demon?" Ham asked fiercely. He had his right arm drawn back, fist clenched.

"I'm good Ham; it's fine," Marrisa rushed to assure him.

Uriel, for his part, chuckled softly. "Well done, young warrior. Your world needs more willing spirits such as you."

"Sorry, Raquel's eyes glow white so I figured a different color meant..." Ham said by way of explanation.

"All of my brethren have slightly different influences on their vessels," Uriel explained. "But if the eyes are any shade of white, silver, gold, or even a light bronze in one case, there's an angel inside. It's the red, yellow, and bright green eyes of which you need be wary."

Moving about the room he was gesturing and muttering under his breath. "We can't stay very long but perhaps Marrisa can fill you in on what has happened today while I finish my warding."

Three minutes later Ham knew the basics and the room was well guarded. "No demonic presence or servant can enter this room now," Uriel informed them. "If they are forced into the room their bodies will die instantly."

"How long will the protection last?" Ham wanted to know.

"It is not the room but you who are warded, young warrior," Uriel informed the gaping teen. "Any room you are in is likewise warded against demonic intrusion."

"And how long will that last?" Ham insisted.

"Until I remove it," Uriel said simply.

SIXTEEN

FOR THE NEXT HOUR THE three women exchanged tidbits of information in hushed tones in the ICU waiting room. Marrisa had made her way back to them and filled Clara/Raquel in on Uriel's doings including her possession. Raquel had likewise filled them in on what she had learned while *outside* Clara's body.

"War is coming, and soon," Raquel informed them solemnly. "There are hordes of demons amassing in the communities surrounding several major metropolitan areas and Oklahoma City is one of the targets. It would appear the *Bible Belt* isn't as secure as local ministers would lead their flocks to believe."

"Are these hordes of demons in cloned bodies like we discussed before?" Pris asked.

"Exactly, and they're being led by their prime supplicant or *zero patient*, as the case were," Raquel replied.

"Prime supplicant? Zero patient?" Marrisa repeated, clearly puzzled.

"The only way a human being may give their body to Lucifer's use is by becoming a supplicant to him; beseeching Satan as a god for guidance and pledging fealty," Raquel explained. "The Center for Disease Control uses the term *Patient Zero* to refer to the first person to become infected in a serious of patient exposures or an epidemic. I wasn't sure which phrase you would more readily understand, so I offered both."

A man in green scrubs with a surgical mask dangling from leads around his neck pushed through the doors to the waiting room. As they were the only people waiting, Marrisa rose and all three turned to face him. His slumped posture and general body language said he did not have good news for them.

"I'm Dr. Pashteen, Chief of Neurology, and I've been overseeing Detective Kratos' treatment," he offered in a mellifluous sing-song cadence. "Frank is comatose and has brain damage from the concussion of the explosion. The brain is a marvelous organ and can heal and reroute itself, given enough time and adequate brain cells in the right areas."

He explained in the way most doctors felt was necessary to share with waiting family. "Unfortunately, the amount of damage his brain has suffered is not only very serious but also in those areas most important to his recovery."

"What does all that mean in layman's terms?" Marrisa asked impatiently.

"I apologize, it is the nature of my job to try to help family members understand what is happening in the best way I know how," he smiled as he glanced at the floor. Raising his head he looked from one set of waiting eyes to the next until he had made eye contact with all three women.

"It means I'm afraid his chances of recovery are very small. We will keep him on life-support for as long as necessary and will do everything we can to aid in his recovery." He turned and began to move away.

Clara gasped and her head rocked backward as if struck but immediately righted herself as her eyes flared silver. Raquel said, "*He will wipe away every tear from their eyes, and death shall be no more, neither shall there be mourning, nor crying, nor pain anymore, for the former things have passed away.*"

"What did you say?" Pris asked her.

Marrisa recognized the passage from her husband Phillip's funeral; it was from the Book of Revelation. Calling out to the retreating form of the neurosurgeon she asked, "Can we see him?"

The doctor turned back to them, embarrassment plain on his face. "Of course you may," he replied. "Please forgive me for not offering right away." He turned to the double-doors, keying them open with a pass card. "Right this way please, or shall I allow you a few moments? Shall I send someone out?"

Raquel spoke quickly before Marrisa could reply. "If you would be so kind, thank you. In about five minutes?"

Dr. Pashteen nodded and allowed the door to close quietly behind him. As soon as the door closed Raquel turned her blazing gaze on the other two. "Frank is the linchpin for all that is to come. We must see to his recovery right away."

"Did you not understand what the doctor just said?" Pris asked incredulously. "He's in a coma and not expected to recover."

"Oh yea of little faith," Raquel replied.

The radio she had picked up off the counter in the kitchen squawked in her bag, and Marrisa's hand dove into her purse to retrieve it.

"I said I need to know if I can let Hamilton Nichols leave the hospital un-escorted. He's being discharged and there's no one here to take him home," the radio announced.

Without hesitation Marrisa held the walkie-talkie up to her mouth and pressed the push-to-talk. "This is Mrs. Benson; I'm in the ICU waiting room with Mrs. Kratos and we are guardians for Hamilton Nichols. Please escort him here and do *not* let him come by himself. Is that clear?"

The radio was silent for several long moments while Pris and Clara both looked at Marrisa with newfound respect for the audacity she had just dis-played. Apparently the police were feeling the same way.

"This is Sergeant McElroy. Are you the same Mrs. Benson who is the moth-er of Priscilla Benson?" he asked.

"I am," she replied.

"How did *you* get to the hospital unescorted? You weren't supposed to leave the residence without effective escort per the lieutenant's explicit directions," he fumed. "And where did you get a police radio?"

"I drove us here in my van for which I have a license and which is equipped to carry not one, but both of the wheelchair users soon to be with me. And Of-ficer Omikawa left the radio," she answered succinctly, with just a little edge in her voice.

"Yes ma'am, I understand," he said, suddenly all cooperation. "I'll personally be escorting Mr. Nichols to the ICU waiting room in short order."

Pris gaped at her mother. "Go Mom," she gushed.

Raquel also nodded her beaming countenance in approval. "These are be-coming desperate times and call for desperate measures."

Three minutes later by her watch Marrisa observed Ham turn the corner from the elevator lobby toward them. A tall, red-haired, muscular policeman with a huge handlebar mustache strode beside him.

"Sergeant McElroy I presume?" Marrisa said, rising and offering her hand.

He shook her hand firmly, maintaining his grip longer than necessary. "I don't know whether to arrest you, hug you, or both," he said, finally releasing her hand.

"I don't know you well enough to hug and why would you feel you could arrest me?" Marrisa replied coolly.

"Why would I feel I could...you mean why would I think I should?" McElroy replied flustered.

"No, I said what I meant," Marrisa smiled. "Perhaps you haven't been briefed on what capabilities our young super heroes have as of yet." She grinned at Ham and then Pris.

"Super heroes? Ah, no ma'am, I don't believe I have," he admitted. "There have been some rumors but I've learned to stick with facts during my 12 years on the force," he informed them.

"Let's just say, unless I wanted to go with you I don't think you could make me," she answered boldly.

Sergeant McElroy was aghast. He had never had anyone appear so utterly confident that he could not exercise his authority over them and it showed plainly. "Perhaps you could enlighten me?" he finished, his voice a mixture of curiosity and something near contempt.

"No, you really don't want me to do that unless you're a good swimmer," Ham replied.

Clara, Priscilla and Marrisa all burst into simultaneous giggles.

"Are you all on drugs?" the sergeant asked. "Did they give you something after the incident at the Kratos residence? I need to call for some additional officers to escort you to a safe location," he finished, reaching for his radio.

Ham glanced at the radio as he drew it from its holster and watched as he pressed the talk pad. "This is Sergeant McElroy. I need six officers to the ICU waiting room forthwith."

He held the radio slightly away from his ear anticipating a reply. When none was forthcoming he repeated his request, twisting the knobs on top in an attempt to get some response. The radio was dead. McElroy tapped the radio against the palm of his beefy hand, turning the power knob off and on several times.

"Huh, it was fully charged when I came on shift two hours ago," he said, more to himself than the others.

Remembering Marrisa had a radio, he looked at her. "Mrs. Benson, I'll need to recover the radio Officer Omikawa gave you," he said, holding out his hand.

"Certainly," Marrisa replied, handing the radio to him. "And I didn't say Omikawa *gave* it to me, I said he left it."

Raquel had been smiling throughout the exchange and was about to speak when McElroy keyed the radio. Nothing happened and he went through the same routine he had with his own. Patrick McElroy wasn't born at night or last night; he smelled a set-up.

"What exactly is going on here?" he asked plaintively.

"Please allow me to demonstrate," Ham offered. The others watched in earnest to see what new skills he might have discovered. "Don't be alarmed, I have no intention of hurting you," he concluded, addressing the now smirking officer.

The radio McElroy had placed in its holster sprang from the leather case and bounced off the ceiling tile overhead, rattling it in its frame. It then made a circuitous loop around the room before coming to a stop two feet in front of the Sergeant's face.

When the shocked policeman reached for the walkie it danced away from his hand as if they were magnetic opposites. Dawn rose on the startled officer's face and he realized the rumors he had heard were at least partially true. The big man stumbled toward a waiting chair and collapsed into it, bouncing it several inches backward.

"So you see I really don't need police protection, I have my own," Marrisa said proudly.

Raquel called the officer by his first name. "Patrick, you're a wonderfully devout man and my Father loves you for your faith. Have faith now that what you see and hear in the near future is all for His good and His will."

The door of a storage closet opened twenty feet down the hall, and Uriel stepped out in his host body. "I heard your call," he said without preamble. "How may I serve?"

It was testament to the bizarre nature of the night that none of the other's were shocked to see the custodian step out of a closet when they had been there for hours and had not seen him go in. Turning to the others, Raquel said, "We must tend to Frank's recovery now; time is slipping away and he must be there to fight with us, or all is lost."

SEVENTEEN

THEY WERE GATHERED in a semi-circle around Frank's bedside holding hands. Clara was at Frank's right holding his hand and Priscilla's. Marrisa stood at the end of the bed holding hands with Priscilla and Uriel. Ham was parked on the other side of the bed at the head holding Frank's left hand in his good right one. Uriel held Ham's limp hand in his strong one.

There had been tears and remonstrations followed by final acceptance of Frank's condition. Each had made some gesture of love or affection toward him individually but Frank had not responded. Finally, Raquel had enough.

"There is no time for anything except faith; the good, strong faith in our Father I know you all have." Looking at them all, she confided. "My brother Uriel and I have great powers by your reckoning. Where we are from all have what you would consider incredible abilities. But our strength is severely muted in these mortal coils. To utilize them fully we would do the host permanent, irreparable damage and this we can never do."

She smiled as she waited for this to sink in; then continued. "We can however, guide you to fully realizing your own innate abilities. Every human has a depth of ability few ever plumb and we need you to do three things. First and foremost, believe you have such abilities."

"Ham and Pris have seen theirs in use, but what has been displayed thus far is only a shining token of the wealth of power they possess." Raquel continued. "Not all have their level of power, in fact few do. Even fewer ever actualize it and for those, it takes decades of concentration and training. You have little of the training and none of the time."

"Be not discouraged, for Our Father has permitted us the great favor of teaching you as quickly as possible," Uriel added. "You must only be willing to focus your minds and energies like you have never done so before. Exclude everything from your awareness. Listen only to the sound of our song and heed the awakening."

"When the power flows into you do not resist it," Raquel concluded. "This is the final and most dangerous part of your emergency training. If you resist the force you may in fact be rendered dumbstruck. It may or may not pass, but you will be of no use to us in the battle to come."

Marrisa cleared her throat. When Raquel met her gaze she asked rather humbly, "Am I to understand we are all to be given special powers or abilities? Because I for one am not even remotely prepared to do so. I'm afraid I'll ruin it for everyone else."

"My apology Marrisa, I neglected to acknowledge only three of you are in training. You are in the circle because of the love and support you offer these three and your energies are not unsubstantial. Rather than deplete you, when the awakening occurs for Priscilla, Hamilton, and even Clara, you will feel like you could take on all-comers."

"That energy will sustain you in the battle at hand. But I must caution you," she said sternly. "Do not under any circumstances break the circle until I tell you to do so. Is that absolutely clear? It must remain intact during the passage or serious injury may occur to all humans in the link."

"Yes, it's clear," Marrisa said softly but firmly.

"Then let us begin," Raquel said, looking at Pris and Ham. "Find a point to focus your gaze upon, somewhere near the center of your natural resting position for your eyes. Keep your eyes open and focused on that spot. It may very well appear to recede into a great distance but do not break your focus. Tell me when you have found your focal point."

First Ham and then Pris indicated they had.

"Now clear your mind of all thought," she continued their instructions in a stern tone. "Do not concern yourselves with any sounds you hear nor with any sights you may think you see. And most of all do not be concerned with anything any of the others do. Maintain your focus and listen only to our song. Are you ready?"

Ham said yes immediately but Pris seemed hesitant. Finally she looked at her mother out of the corner of her eye and said, "Mom, can I have a kiss for luck?"

Releasing Uriel's hand, Marrisa turned to where she was directly in front of her daughter. "You've got this kiddo. You've always been so much stronger than you realize." Kissing her daughter lightly on the lips, she stood back in place and took up Uriel's hand again.

"Ready," Pris announced.

Raquel looked to Uriel and nodding. Both angels turned their faces to the ceiling, closed their eyes, and opened their mouths.

What issued forth sounded like no song or music any had ever heard. Then it began to sound like every song they'd ever heard which had made their hearts dance and their toes want to tap. As the song progressed it spiraled from a low register through higher octaves. The sound was as if a multitude of voices, many thousands of them, were humming or sighing notes and sounds but not words.

For Ham, he saw himself running across a meadow chasing a spotted dog. He was laughing and calling its name. For Pris, she was flying in a swing and her father was below her pushing her ever higher. Tears of joy streaked both young people's faces and their breathing turned rapid and shallow.

The song continued into registers most people cannot hear and then suddenly the room was still and silent. Marrisa at first thought something had gone wrong or that it was over. But she remembered Raquel's admonition to not release her grip until told to do so. Looking around she saw both angels still had their heads tilted back. Their throats worked as if singing or speaking but no sound emerged.

Ham and Pris were still focused on whatever spots they had chosen and then it dawned on her. *They're in registers I can't hear*, she thought in amazement. Closing her eyes, Marrisa willed her love for Priscilla and growing admiration for Ham to flow down her arms and out into the circle. She imagined it was a powerful electrical current and she was using it to light the faces of her loved ones.

Softly at first and then with increasing volume, the song descended back through the registers to where Marrisa could here, this time painfully so. The volume was louder than any concert she'd ever been to as a young, single college student and she had to physically command herself not to move her hands to cover her ears. Instead she hunched her shoulders and bent her knees slightly, doing whatever she could to cover her ears without breaking the circle.

Abruptly it ended. Her ears rang as if an explosion had happened nearby, and the sudden absence of sound rocked her on her feet. She clung desperately to Uriel's hand, simultaneously hoping she wasn't breaking her daughter's from squeezing too hard.

"Hamilton and Priscilla; without breaking the circle, gaze upon each other and seal your bond," Uriel commanded.

Ham turned his head toward the foot of the bed and Pris turned her gaze to meet his. Their eyes flashed brilliant white, then molten silver, before returning to their natural colors. The expressions on their faces spoke of bedazzlement and euphoria. Raquel now spoke and her command sounded like thunder in the room. "Ham, command Frank to awaken." Her tone brooked no nonsense or resistance and Ham knew too well how much she knew of his abilities, even if he did not.

"Frank, time to wake up, Lieutenant," Ham said congenially.

Clara spasmed on Frank's right and her grip faltered on Priscilla's. Her eyes went opaque white, as if she had severe cataracts. Everyone knew Raquel had, at least momentarily they hoped, left the room. And just as quickly Clara's eyes flared brilliant white and Raquel looked again to Ham.

"Hamilton Nichols, I did not say invite him to wake up, I said *command* him," she bellowed. Cringing from the force of the command, Ham shuddered before turning his full gaze and attention to Frank's somnolent face.

"Frank Kratos, I command you to wake up," he shouted in his most authoritative voice.

Everyone held their breath, waiting. Marrisa was the first to exhale audibly. One by one the rest let out their pensive breath; nothing had happened.

There were different expressions around the room; Raquel seemed only mildly disappointed while Priscilla was crying openly. Uriel was gazing at him blankly while Marrisa's look was a combination of disappointment and pity. Ham remembered then how Uriel had called him a young warrior. Summoning the inner peace and calm he had developed over a lifetime of challenges and setbacks while remembering the joy he had greeted each new day with before this had all begun, he felt a different sense of the world descend upon him.

No one had broken the circle as yet, and Ham firmed his grip on Frank's left hand as he spoke. "Frank, wake up. We have much to do and we need you."

For several breathless moments no one stirred. Then Frank's right hand twitched against his wife's and his eyelids fluttered. A deep intake of air resonated through the room and Frank sighed as if he had just awakened from a restful night's sleep. His eyes fluttered open and he looked around the circle of faces, finally lighting on Clara's.

Smiling sleepily he said, "How's my girl?"

"Hallelujah," shouted Uriel, but Raquel had given over the vessel to Clara.

"My darling, I'm so happy to see you back," she cried.

Marrisa and Priscilla had both simultaneously begun to sob in great gasps of joy, and Ham's shouted "yes" reverberated against the walls. Every face, including the angels, was tear-streaked.

Puzzled, Frank became aware of his surrounding; the hospital room, the leads and wire, tubes and bandages. "Who died?" he asked innocently.

EIGHTEEN

IT TOOK THE BETTER part of two hours to fill Frank in on all that had transpired during the short period he had been unconscious. Near the end of the chaotic conversation in which everyone finished everyone else's sentences and talked over each other, Frank finally broke in. He had been lying quietly trying to soak in all the amazing facts being poured into his brain by a fire hose of information.

"Who's this guy?" he asked, pointing at Uriel.

"I'm Carl, de head custodian heah at de hospital," he explained. "And dis heah's..." he started, making sure Frank was still looking straight at him. Carl's eye flared golden and Uriel said, "My name is Uriel. Carl has graciously allowed me to manifest in his vessel and Raquel is my sister. It was through our concerted efforts we were able to teach Hamilton and Priscilla how to heal your many and grievous wounds."

Frank's mouth dropped open and his heart monitor rhythm changed from a gentle waltz to a salsa. Within seconds, the door burst open and the charge nurse stepped in, sliding to a halt when she saw the group gathered around her patient's bed.

"Who are all you people? What are you doing in my room? You can't all be in here at once..." she was about to continue when she saw Frank was awake. "How long has he been awake? *Who's in charge here?*" she nearly bellowed.

She spun to leave the room, apparently intent on calling security, but a motion from Raquel had her spin back around. "I know you," the nurse said quietly as if recognizing an old friend. "You're Frank's wife. I saw you on television when you helped Frank find that sick man who was hurting those young boys."

"Yes, I'm Clara the Clairvoyant," she said with a self-deprecating grin.

The nurse's grin changed to a grimace as she asked Clara, "Who are all these people? Did Dr. Pashteen permit you to visit because of Frank's...condition?" she faltered, not sure yet how to reconcile a lucid, communicating patient with one she had been told was unofficially being classified as terminally brain-dead.

"Yes they're all friends of the family. I'm sure you'd like to meet them all, but don't you think Dr. Pashteen needs to know Frank is awake?" Clara suggested pointedly.

"Well yes, but I don't think he'll want all of you in here when he comes to examine the detective," she concurred, still vacillating between her overwhelming instinct to revert to her years of training and the influence being wielded by Raquel.

"Sister, let her be," Uriel commanded softly.

The nurse looked questioningly at Uriel before turning toward the door. "I'll need you to clear the room by the time the doctor arrives," she called over her shoulder.

Frank looked at Uriel and asked, "You're an Archangel as well?"

At Uriel's nod, he looked at his wife. And you're his sister Raquel?"

At her nod he glanced around the room at the others. "Any additional angels, Archangels, demons, unicorns, pixies, or other supernatural beings in here I should know about?"

Ham barked a short laugh. "Good one Frank."

"I'm serious young man," he replied deadpan. "If you ask them outright they have to tell you."

All heads turned to Uriel, who smiled and nodded. "He is correct, although that's not a fact we like to make common knowledge. How did you come by this information?" Uriel asked Frank.

Dr. Pashteen chose that moment to enter the room. "I'll need you all to leave please. Carl, what are *you* doing in here?" the doctor stopped and asked, spying the custodian who stood out from the group because of his uniform and size.

Before Carl could respond, Frank took charge. "Doctor, I need you to discharge me right away and certify I'm capable of returning to duty. There are many bad people in our city who intend serious harm or death to all these people as well as the the general populace, and I'm in charge of the investigation. Let's get to it, shall we?"

The others had slowly filtered out of the room with Carl leading the way. Clara was the last in the line and stopped near the door. "I'll ask the nurse where I should go to take care of whatever paperwork is required just to speed things along," she said before rolling out of the room.

Dr. Pashteen had started to rebuff her statement when Frank called after her, "You do that sweetheart. This shouldn't take long."

The doctor turned back to Frank and began. "We must run several tests to confirm your requests detective, and I won't be able to order them until the morning," he said, pulling a pen light from his breast pocket. "I'll get the paperwork started as soon as I finish my preliminary examination." He paused, flicking the light into Frank's eyes one at a time to check dilation and response.

"And if all is well you should be going home tomorrow afternoon. Please watch my finger with just your eyes, keeping your head stationary," he requested while holding up his right index finger. Frank dutifully did as requested and when he finished, Dr. Pashteen looked puzzled. "This is highly irregular," he began, picking up Frank's hands in his own and placing his first two fingers against Frank's palms. "Squeeze my fingers with equal pressure from both hands," he directed.

The exam took another 10 minutes, with the doctor using every physical examination protocol he could remember to check Frank's neurological function. He could tell by the growing impatience on Frank's face that he would have to fight to keep his patient any longer.

"I cannot in all good conscience release you tonight Frank, even though you seem remarkably recovered," he offered, puzzled at his patient's astounding condition. "Please, slowly, stand up at the side of the bed. If you experience any dizziness, lightheadedness, or dimming of vision; sit back down immediately." Frank did as asked and was clear-eyed and focused when he met the doctor's gaze.

"Raise your right hand over your head and hold your left hand out in front of you," the doctor directed. When Frank did so with ease the doctor continued.

"Slowly raise your right foot off the floor, just an inch or so." And again Frank easily complied.

"Place your left hand over your navel and your right hand flat on top of your head," was the next test.

"Shall I rub my stomach and pat my head?" Frank asked sharply, doing so as he asked.

"Or shall I do the Hokey Pokey and turn myself around?" he continued, doing this and twisting his IV line around his body in the process.

"Perhaps I should perform some light calisthenics?" Frank growled, holding his hands out at his sides and spreading his feet shoulder-width apart. "Side-straddle hop?"

"No, no, detective; please stop," the doctor said in a panic. "You're twisting your IV line and you may crimp it or even pull it out."

"Well I can fix that," Frank said, his patience exhausted. Reaching down with his left hand he pulled the IV line from his right forearm, dripping a stream of clear fluid across the floor as he dropped the rubber line and needle onto the bed.

"Doctor, I've never felt better in my entire life and I'm not just saying that. I feel like I'm 25 years old again and I don't hurt anywhere," he fumed. "Did I have any bruising, lacerations, or broken bones when I was admitted?" The doctor reached for the chart at the foot of the bed and, keeping one eye on Frank, glanced over the attached forms.

"You had bruising on your back on the left side, a large contusion on your right shoulder, what should be a bruised right kidney or worse and a laceration requiring five stitches on your right knee. We're still waiting for the lab to tell us if there's any blood in your urine. Speaking of which, I should call someone to remove your catheter if you're absolutely determined to leave."

The look on Frank's face spoke volumes, and he reached under the gown to feel for himself. "Can I just pull it out as well or is there some special process?" He asked cautiously. Apparently, Frank wasn't as ready to yank out a catheter as he was an IV line.

Dr. Pashteen sighed. "Just pull gently and slowly with steady pressure," he started but hurriedly finished. "As soon as I get a clamp to close the line."

Once clamped the collection bag and line were placed on the bed as well and Frank wasted no time disrobing. Looking down his length, his gaze fell on his unblemished right knee. "Five stitches, huh?" he quipped.

Dr. Pashteen wasn't listening. Frank was turned partially away, whether out of modesty or circumstance was uncertain. The doctor could see Frank's left torso; and he could also see it was complete free of any mark or blemish. Walking around him, Dr. Pashteen touched his right lower back where his kidney would be and pressed gently.

"Any pain or discomfort here?" the doctor asked softly.

"Nope," Frank replied. Then he reached behind himself, placing his hands flat in the small back. Arching backward he laughed. "I haven't been able to do that in eight years," he chuckled in amazement.

"I'm a doctor and I believe in science," Dr. Pashteen spoke softly, almost reverently. "But I'm also a man of faith and I believe I've just witnessed my first miracle healing. There is no outward evidence of any injury on your body and even the stitches are gone from your knee."

Eyes wide in amazement he reached and flung down the sheet on the bed, covering the collection bag. He almost knocked the IV line onto the floor from where it lay on the top sheet in a spreading stain of nutritive fluids. There on the stark white sheets were five tiny black wads of thread, still tied in perfect surgical knots.

FRANK WAS DRESSED IN the clothes he had been wearing during the fight at his house and standing downstairs at the ER entrance 25 minutes later. His clothes were much worse for the wear but he was more concerned with his missing sidearm.

"They told me they gave it to Sergeant McElroy but I have no way to reach him, if he's even still in the hospital," he informed no one in particular.

Frank might have thought he was finished with surprises for the night but another one was forthcoming. Marrisa reached into her shoulder bag and pulled out the radio which Ham had caused to fly around the room earlier. They hadn't told Frank that part yet.

"Sgt. McElroy, this is Mrs. Benson. Are you still in the hospital? Lieutenant Kratos would like to speak to you."

The radio crackled to life immediately. "I'm on my way to the ICU right now," was the excited reply.

"He's not in ICU, he's being discharged. We're in the ER; could you meet us there please?" A double break on the squelch was the only reply.

After several seconds when Marrisa raised the radio to repeat her request, Frank held his hand up. "That double squawk was the standard response for affirmative." He held his hand out and Marrisa handed him the radio willingly; almost eagerly.

"Pat, have you still got my service revolver?" Frank asked.

"Yes sir, I have it on me. I'll be there in two minutes," he replied.

"Don't kill yourself getting here," Frank said, nervously glancing around the room at realizing his faux pas; but everyone was laughing.

NINETEEN

"SOMEONE'S BEEN BUSY," Pris observed as the van doors opened in the Kratos' driveway.

"How's that?" Frank asked from the front seat of his van.

Clara had released her chair from its locks and turned to face the open door of the other van. They had left Carl at the hospital with the promise he would join them after his shift. Frank's miraculous recovery was enough of a flashing neon sign illuminating odd happenings without the head custodian being seen leaving with that same patient.

"The front door is closed," Ham interjected from his place where his chair was tied down behind Pris in Marrisa's van.

"Well shouldn't it be?" Frank asked quizzically.

"No, when we left the front door was laying on the floor in the living room," Marrisa finished.

"Ah, the explosion," Frank supplied. "The one in which I was almost killed and Marrisa in turn killed a top-level demon," he finished as if discussing a slight change in the weather.

"Uriel vanquished Berith back to the realm of the condemned," Raquel supplied in turn.

"It is nearly impossible for any of my Father's children to be killed," Clara informed him. "Only He can actually cause them to cease to exist. This is why Father had to condemn them to the *other place*." As she spoke the term Clara's body literally quivered in disgust.

"So your brothers and sisters are immortal and invulnerable, kind of like Superman?" Ham quipped.

"We don't use terms like immortal because we have no reference," Raquel responded. "We are in fact eternal; our Father made us so when He created us out of the essence of the universe, which He himself created by His will."

"This is probably not the right time to ask but, here goes. If your Father, He whom we call God, created the universe and all which is in it; does that mean you don't live in this universe?" Ham asked expectantly.

"You are such a bright young man!" Raquel beamed enthusiastically. "Even my Father's prophets took years to grasp this as a concept."

"The prophets didn't have comic books," Pris snarked.

Ignoring her quip, Raquel turned to Hamilton very seriously and asked, "And where do you suppose we live instead?"

"Well gee, if I had to guess I'd say....another dimension?" Ham answered hesitantly.

"Pin a prize on that young man's chest," Raquel crowed.

"Ah, I think you mean pin a medal on my chest? Or give me a prize?" Ham offered.

"Yes, yes, your colloquialisms continue to elude me occasionally," Raquel admitted. "Regardless, we in fact live in a dimension which is nearly pure energy. Father used a small fraction of that energy to create this universe in this dimension."

"He was hoping it too would be eternal but alas, it allowed decay to enter when my oldest brother was jealous of Father doting on His new creations." Raquel's face fell for a moment remembering her love for her fallen brother. "Lucifer said they were weak and frail, and easily swayed. Father reminded us all then that our charge was to watch over all of His creation for as long as it continued to exist."

She paused and a distant look stole across her face. "It was part of the cause for the great battle, where Brother and Sister fought Brother and Sister for dominion of our realm. Father could have easily stopped it but chose to let it play out to test our resolve and see how much we had learned in the eons since we had been created. He was disappointed in Lucifer and many of his followers, so He banished them to the *other place* for all eternity." Again, Clara's frail frame shuddered in revulsion.

"Your reaction leads us to believe it's a pretty terrible place," Frank remarked.

"It is a place of no beauty and no light. It is eternal darkness and my Brothers and Sisters grope about blindly. They call to us unceasingly across the chasm which none of us can span, and it wears on us." Raising her head Raquel looked at each one of them in turn. "That is until recently when some of *your* brothers and sisters began calling to them in the pit of darkness; inviting them into your existence."

Shaking her head, she continued the tale. "Who among them is strong enough to resist surcease of their torment, if only a brief respite from such eternal torture? And so they come into your realm, with twisted spirits bent on revenge against our Father for their rejection. They cannot come unless invited and they have no influence while here, yet they would destroy your very existence, were they capable."

"But if they can't have any influence in this plane of existence, how is it Berith was able to fight Uriel?" Pris asked curiously.

"Just like angels, as you call them, can have almost no influence in this plane, so neither can the fallen ones," Raquel replied. "But those of the prime essence like us, those of Father's original creations; we can wield words of power in this realm."

"I don't understand; I thought God created all the angels?" Pris replied.

"Actually, Father taught all my Brothers and Sisters how to make imitations of ourselves so we would not be lonely," Uriel interjected. "After the first ten million of your years, life amongst the few we were became boring and repetitive. Those which we created you know as angels."

"How many of prime essence did God originally create?" Ham asked insistently.

"There were originally 48 children of our Father, and only one has ever actually been annihilated by Him; he was Qemuel," she concluded sadly. "After that Father swore to never destroy another of us; thus the banishment. But that is a long story and for another time."

"So how do we ever hope to stop them?" Marrisa asked fearfully.

"Understand this," Raquel said firmly. "The vessels they possess are still just as mortal as ever. If you do anything to them you would to any mortal they will be cast back into the pit. Only the original creations can resist such lethal forces, and not entirely. Total destruction of the host can cast them down as well. It is usually only one of my Brothers and Sisters of the Realm who can do so."

"Let me make sure I've got this straight," Frank cut in. "If it's just a demon, one of the creatures of the pit, we can send them back by killing the vessel. But if it's a higher-level demon you have to do it?"

"Not exactly," Raquel replied. "I said you could send them back by destroying the vessel. Doing sufficient damage so they cannot repair the vessel before it enters into decay."

"How long is that?" Frank asked insistently.

"How long can your bodies exist without breathing?" she asked in return.

"The common school of thought is the brain begins to die after about 4-5 minutes without oxygen," Frank explained. "There have been reported cases of it being much longer, especially when the body is frozen or seriously chilled. But 4-5 minutes is a good starting point."

"Hey, speaking of freezing, it's really cold out here. And I'm really freaking out with all this killing and decay talk about other people," Pris rejoined. "Plus I feel really exposed, sitting out here in the van," she finished. "No insult intended on your abilities," she added, looking at Raquel.

"None taken and Priscilla is right," she said. "We should move inside and continue this training. There is scarce time and much to impart."

Marrisa, who had been sitting on the floor of the van next to her daughter, lifted her head up and looked behind Frank's van.

"Speaking of security, someone's out there."

TWENTY

FRANK WAS OUT OF THE driver's seat like a shot as Marrisa fumbled in her bag. Weapon at high ready he rounded the corner of the van and came face-to-face with Omikawa.

"Whoa, easy Lieutenant," he squealed, holding his hands up alongside his head.

"Sing out next time, that's a good way to earn an extra hole," Frank barked gruffly.

"Sorry, I've been sitting over in the patrol car watching y'all since you arrived," Omikawa explained. "I was beginning to worry something was wrong after y'all sat here for five minutes and didn't get out."

Frank always had to stifle a grin when Jason Omikawa spoke. He looked every bit the Japanese heritage he claimed but he had been born and raised in Chickasha and had the "Okie" drawl down pat. Seeing an Asian face say *y'all* made him smile inside.

"Why are you here?" Frank asked heatedly. "I heard you were pretty messed up in the first assault. Why aren't you home resting? Aren't you on sick leave?"

Omikawa knew better than to interrupt Frank so he hesitated when Frank stopped talking. Seeing he wasn't going to say any more he answered all the questions. "I'm here because I requested to be here even though it's not officially *light duty*, which I've been cleared for. Nothing broken, just some sprains and pulled muscles."

"Sprains and pulls can take longer to heal than breaks, we both know that," Frank chastised. "Who'd you sweet-talk to get released for limited and again, why here; why not a desk?"

"Because I want first crack at the bast.." Omikawa caught himself, stepping sideways and eyeing the young people emerging from the vans. When he looked at Frank again he was having trouble containing his mirth. "I want the bad guys who did this to me and you, LT. And speaking of light duty, someone needs to call the desk sergeant. He's put the word out you were comatose and had a low chance of recovering."

When Frank puffed up to lay into him again Omikawa quickly added, "That is to say I'm seriously glad you weren't hurt, sir. Your clothes are trashed but there doesn't appear to be a mark on you. Shouldn't *you* be on light duty, sir?" he finished, still grinning like a fiend.

"What are you *grinning* at?" Frank growled, stepping between the two vans.

Marrisa was crouched on the ground in front of her daughter's chair which was still in the van. She held a massive revolver clutched tightly in both hands and its barrel trembled as she pointed it in his direction. The weapon was overtly menacing, black and shiny. The opening of the long, vent-ribbed barrel looked to be the size of a baseball. Hamilton had moved his chair so he could see around the van's sliding door and had his arm cocked back as if to throw his own ball.

Frank looked at Ham, grinned and said, "Don't shoot."

Then he looked to Marrisa and still grinning, asked, "Where'd you get the hand cannon?"

Marrisa sheepishly lowered the heavy gun to her thigh as she rose slowly. "It was Phillip's and he taught me how to use it," she replied, wiggling it around. "I just never felt the need to carry it until now."

"I'm guessing you had that in your bag at the hospital?" Frank asked, still smiling. He nodded approvingly when he saw her index finger couched alongside the cylinder and not on the trigger.

"Oh, no. I would never carry a gun into a hospital where my daughter's boyfriend and one of my new best friends were being treated for life-threatening wounds caused by rampaging demons in human form," she replied acerbically. "That would be illegal."

Looking at the others he said, "Let's make our way inside. It looks like we have a lot of discussion to finish."

ONCE THEY WERE ALL settled in the living room Frank turned to Omikawa and resumed their previous conversation. "Who's in the patrol with you?"

"I'm solo," Jason replied. "We all are now that more craziness has begun. There aren't *any* patrols out with two officers on board. That's one of the reasons I'm still on duty; we need every able-bodied officer we have. The Captain's already called for mutual aid from Blanchard, Anadarko, and Rush Springs. OKC already has their hands full."

"I think you'd better bring us all up to speed on what you just said," Frank ordered, looking lost as he gazed across his companions.

"Sir?" Omikawa questioned. "These civilians, as nice of folks as they are, and thank you ma'am for allowing me to rest here for a while," he said in an aside to Clara, who smiled and nodded. "I don't think they need to know what's happening. It's...well, LT, it's kinda nuts."

Frank sighed the heavy expulsion of a man who has become accustomed to relying on himself and is now being required to put too much faith in others. "Sit down Jason and I'll try to be brief. Hold your questions until I'm finished," he said. Turning to the others he continued, "Please don't finish my sentences for me. I know there are details I'm leaving out but he just needs to know the essentials for now."

In just under five minutes Frank filled in all the gaps from the evening's activities including his resurrection at the hospital. When he finished, Jason sat speechless. After a minute, he cleared his throat to bring the shocked young officer back to himself, then said, "Your turn."

"There's rioting in the city," he said, referring to Oklahoma City. In most parts of the state, *The City* meant OKC unless you were in the northeast, then it was Tulsa.

"They've put out an all call for every available peace officer, including reserves, court officers, the Feds, game wardens, OHP, the DA's office; you name it. There doesn't seem to be any pattern to the riots, just uncontrolled violence. Cars turned over and set on fire, stores broken into and looted, gangs roaming the streets robbing and beating people; single women..." he paused, swallowing hard.

"Well, you get the idea. The Governor's even talking about activating and *arming* the National Guard." Jason had grown pale during his recitation but now his color flared. "Gangs are working *with other gangs* and there have been a lot of *shots fired* calls coming in. There were no triggers anyone can identify; it was just like someone flipped a switch and all the bad guys went crazy at once."

"It has begun," Raquel whispered into the silence which threatened to deafen everyone in the room. "We're out of time."

"Wait, you said angels were here to help but they need a willing vessel, right?" Jason blurted. When Raquel nodded Jason said, "I'm willing; take me. I'm still in pretty good shape and maybe, you know like you said, they can fix me up so I'm ready for action?"

Clara eyes darkened and then flew open as she shrugged, looking first at Jason then around the room. "There has been an angel *all-call*," she informed them, copying Jason's term. "Watcher's from all over the planet are reporting similar sequences of events. Apparently this is an onslaught of global proportions and it is well coordinated. The entire planet is rioting."

TWENTY-ONE

FRANK WAS ON HIS RADIO getting status updates from any available sources. First responders were answering calls for house and car fires, vicious beatings, robberies, and multiple cases of gang rape. Many citizens were armed and barricaded inside their own homes.

The calls for vandalism, breaking and entering, and simple theft where no one was assaulted or injured were being told no one was coming. 911 call center operators told these fortunate ones to take precautions against additional attacks by moving to shelters with large groups of people. Churches and synagogues were opening and the faithful were pouring inside, seeking shelter from this most unusual storm.

"Yes we'll use them," Frank was saying on the radio. "I know every one of those guys; they're all either retired law enforcement, prior military, or at least CLEET certified," he said. The second reference was to the Oklahoma Council on Law Enforcement Education and Training. The first was to one of the local chapters of self-defense citizen organizations.

"Send them to the churches and synagogues in teams of four; full gear. Many of them are as well equipped as we are. Tell them to set guards at the front doors and lock and barricade all the other entrances. And make sure they know that nobody fires a weapon except in direct self-defense of immediate threat to life," Frank admonished. "Make *sure* they acknowledge that even though I know they already understand the drill."

As the radio squawked with yet another call he saw his wife's eyes flare bright white. "Stand by," he spoke into the radio before turning his full attention to Raquel.

"This is unheard of but these are unprecedented times," she said carefully. "My brother Camael, whom your world knows as the Archangel of strength, courage and war has agreed to accept Jason's offer. Jason, be certain this is what you want. The effects can be... alarming at the very least."

First Jason just nodded but then he spoke to ensure there was no misunderstanding. "I'm sure and I'm ready. What do I need to do?"

"Just sit back, relax and open your heart to Camael," she replied. "I sense you have a warrior's spirit and will suit him well."

Everyone was expecting something dramatic and they were all slightly disappointed. Jason closed his eyes and relaxed visibly twitching once, and then again. His right leg jerked and his face contorted into a grimace for a moment, but he didn't cry out. When he opened his eyes they shone a bright, light bronze.

"Hello sister," Camael spoke. It was still Jason's voice but there were richer undertones of power in the timber.

"Brother, tell us what transpires," Raquel asked immediately.

"This is no simple outbreak nor is it a random testing of our responses. This is an *uprising*," he finished harshly. "As most we can tell, Azazel, Harut, Allocen, Mastema, Asmoday, Balberith, and Leviathan are involved and Amom awaits. They're all being led by Abaddon."

"Not Amom, too?" Raquel whispered, tears forming in her eyes.

"Yes sister, I fear it is true," Camael replied softly.

"But how is that possible?" she insisted. "Allocen has influence as does Balberith, and Asmoday's influence is already most obvious from all the...sexual assaults. But Amom cannot activate his legions without the Gates of the Pit being opened, and Maalik stands guard there with his nineteen."

"Each of those I've just mentioned now walk this planet and influence crowds of weak-minded humans into becoming uncontrolled mobs," Camael replied. "All across the planet the seven gates are being assaulted by these mobs, each led by one of the seven. The fights in this country are going on in Pennsylvania right now and in a town called Hell's Gate, TX. It is some 300 miles from here."

He paused, shaking his head in a very real human expression of bafflement. "As more humans surrender to their more base instincts and answer the call for violence, more are willing to allow possession. At some point this will no longer be just rioting and mob action; they will succeed in overwhelming at least one of the gates. Should one fall it will be only a matter of time until they all do so unless these mobs are stopped now."

Looking forlornly around their company, he concluded with, "And I fear we are not enough for the likes of these denizens of the darkness."

"I have so many questions I don't know where to begin," Marrisa started. "But I do know this; I'll do whatever I must to prevent that from happening, including allowing an angel to use my vessel."

"Jason has asked to speak to you directly Marrisa," Camael said.

The bronze glow in his eyes extinguished and Jason spoke. "Ma'am, you need to know that what we were talking about earlier is true in reverse. The only way for one of the demons to defeat one of the angels is to kill their vessel."

He paused for a moment to let that register. "Now I don't have any family except my parents and they'd miss me sorely. But they knew that risk was there when I put on this uniform. You have a daughter to think about and she needs you more than most kids need a parent. I just wanted to make sure you're aware of that."

Marrisa bowed her head and seemed to be carefully weighing the information, but when her head came back up she was smiling. "That may be the first time I actually felt like God heard my prayer, because he answered me. Who is Sariel besides an Archangel?"

Jason's eye flared bronze, and Raquel's head snapped into focus on Marrisa. "You have spoken with the Father," she breathed. "What has He told you what about Sariel?"

"He told me Sariel understands the gravity of our dire situation and is willing to join in the fight using me as his vessel," she said. The sharp gasp from Priscilla had Marrisa turning to her daughter immediately. "Sariel is an Archangel and because of that, I as his vessel will be much harder to kill. In fact," she smiled convincingly, "I'll be almost invulnerable. Apparently, Sariel packs a lot of punch."

"Indeed he does," replied Raquel. "He is one of the original seven and is the equal of any Archdemon of the Pit. Many of us feel he is even Lucifer's equal. He is called *the Angel of Eternity and Trembling* and he has primordial powers. Father sends him into battle reluctantly and it has been over 2,000 years since he last strode the earth."

"It is good our brother Sariel joins the fray. With his guidance we may yet succeed," Camael said with a concerned look.

"What is it brother?" Raquel asked.

"If Sariel is willing to fight, you know the level of his restorative powers," he said. "And as Priscilla's injuries were man-made, Sariel may in fact be able to restore her condition. He's also well known for his protective powers."

"No," Marrisa shouted. "I will not allow you to put my daughter in harm's way."

"Mom, you just said you'd be almost invulnerable and if they can fix me; *how can you not let them*?" Priscilla was crying and nearly screaming at the end. "But you can put yourself in harm's way without considering where that leaves me? How is that right?"

Marrisa sat and stared at Priscilla for several long seconds before rushing across the room to drop to her knees beside her chair. Hugging her fiercely she sobbed, "I'm sorry baby. I wasn't thinking of you, I was thinking of myself." Smiling through her tears she said, "I don't like it but this may be the miracle we've been praying for."

Turning to Camael, Marrisa wiped her face and said, "Will you ask Sariel if he's willing to do that and if he thinks he can; heal her I mean?"

"I shall, and if you're still willing to be an angel vessel there are others waiting, in fact anticipating, involvement," Camael replied.

"Bored to tears after millions of years, huh?" Ham said. He had been sitting quietly throughout the entire exchange and everyone had basically forgotten he was there. "If there are others who want a host I'm more than willing, especially if it fixes me," he concluded.

"Hamilton I'm so sorry," Raquel smiled gently. "Your condition is the way God made you; only He can change that. He has a higher plan for you I believe."

The look on Ham's face was heartbreaking. The compounding facts of Priscilla having her injuries healed, Frank being resurrected, Jacob being made right, and even Marrisa getting into the fight was more than he could stand. He spun his chair around and headed through the kitchen and down the hall.

Marrisa started after him but Pris stopped her. "Let me Mom," she pleaded. When Marrisa nodded Pris wheeled after Ham.

"So when does Azrael make his appearance?" Marrisa asked, sitting down and getting comfortable.

"How do you know of Azrael?" Raquel asked dumbfounded.

"Your Father and I had quite the conversation," Marrisa replied. "He told me of how all which just happened might, and He said Azrael and I would be a good fit."

TWENTY-TWO

"YOU MUST ACCOMPANY me to Texas," Camael said to Marrisa.

"Wait, I thought we were going to Hellam Township, Pennsylvania?" she replied.

When you were going to welcome Sariel, yes," he replied. "But now that Priscilla has accepted him into her vessel he is needed there, while you and I must rush to the defense of Hell's Gate."

"But I don't understand. Why can't Priscilla and I go one place as Azrael and Sariel and you and Carl go the other?" Marrisa insisted.

"These are Sariel's decisions. He is the most military-minded of us all but we need martial experience with us as well, so Azrael is the obvious choice. He has not the power I command," Camael explained patiently.

"Uriel and Sariel are both Archangels, and Sariel is Father's Commander. Their powers are more needed in Hellam than in Texas right now so this is where we all must go." The last was spoken in an *I've explained myself now so no more argument* tone of voice and Marrisa knew there was no point in further discussion.

"We'll be joined by Hofniel, the Father's favorite soldier, Arariel, who cures stupidity, and Hemah, the Angel of Wrath," Camael explained their assignments. "Uriel and Sariel will have Cassiel, Father's Anger and Speed, Ariel, Father's Lion, and Adriel, the Primary angel of Death. They go against Abaddon the Destroyer and his mob of angry humans."

Ham had not returned from the back of the house but there was suddenly a great shout from that direction. All present except Clara turned for the hallway just as Priscilla cartwheeled into the room.

"Mom, Mom, Mom," she exclaimed. "Look, I'm fixed. I'm whole again. I can walk and jump and...everything," she shouted while demonstrating each action physically.

A knock came on the front door and Frank's hand snaked toward his revolver before sheepishly realizing the level of power in the room. If three

Archangels and the angel of destruction couldn't stop what might threaten them, his revolver surely wouldn't. Going to the door he opened it to find Carl standing on the stoop.

"Hello Carl, or is it Uriel?" Frank said, stepping back to allow him entry.

"Carl is resting now, I'm afraid all this excitement has been a bit much for him," Uriel explained. "And I've brought company."

Sergeant McElroy strode in behind Uriel accompanied by a man and woman Frank had never met. Tamping down his suspicion he waited for Uriel to make the introductions.

"This is the Angel Hemah," Uriel said, indicating McElroy.

"And this is the Angel Hofniel," he said indicating a well-built young man with quick, cat-like mannerisms.

"This fine young woman is the vessel for my welcome Sister Arariel," he said indicating the last of the party.

Frank looked at Hemah for a moment before simply saying, "The Angel of Wrath, huh? Most of the newbies on the force would already agree," he said with a smile.

The light in McElroy's eye dimmed momentarily and McElroy said, "And when we're done with this they still will."

Turning to the young woman Frank asked, "So who are you when you're not hosting an angel who cures stupidity?"

Plain, clear human eyes regarded him for a cool moment before her crisp voice said, "I'm Sharon Caruthers and I'm a Junior High School principal." The grin which erupted on her face told everyone she appreciated the great irony of the situation as well as they did.

The young man locked eyes with Frank for a moment and said, "We've never met but I have great respect for you, Lieutenant. My kid brother was one of the young boys you rescued from the pedophile no one else had been able to catch. I'm Daniel Santos and I'm a Navy Seal."

"Thank you Daniel, I'm glad we found your brother Fernando in time but I had lots of help," Frank said indicating Clara. "And I'll bet Hofniel is chomping at the bit to give you a test drive."

Golden light flared in Daniel's eyes and he laughed. "We've had several interesting conversations already regarding certain techniques I promise to teach him."

Frank wondered who was teaching whom but didn't have the time to ask. As he looked across the room he noticed Marrisa and Priscilla were still locked in a warm embrace. They seemed to be whispering to each other.

"We need to leave right away, time is of the essence," Camael said taking charge of his team.

"Take my sedan, it's full of gas and should take you the 300 miles easily. Use the lights and siren if required," Frank offered to Jason. "I'll get another vehicle."

"I'll be leaving mine here," Jason replied. "You can take it to the airport."

"Actually we have Carl's station wagon," Uriel said. "The police vehicle may be needed, so we'll take the wagon to the airport where we're all catching the red-ass to Philadelphia."

Several people laughed and Uriel looked puzzled.

"Catching the red-*eye* is an airplane ride, catching the red-ass is what we're all about to do," Priscilla shared. "Come on, I'll explain it in the car."

In less than three minutes the house was empty except for Frank, Ham, and Clara.

Raquel had left the building again and neither of them had any idea when she would return. Frank stepped back and closed the door, turning to Clara with a sigh of relief. She was shaking her head and Frank went to her side.

"What is it?" he asked earnestly.

"Ham is inconsolable," she replied. "I can feel his enmity growing with each passing second and its misplaced target is God. Raquel has asked her Father to speak with him but so far, nothing has happened."

"Maybe I can talk to him," Frank said hopefully.

"I certainly hope so," Clara replied. "It hurts my heart to see him so morose."

HAM WAS SEATED FACING the picture window in Clara's bedroom. The lights were out and the scant illumination from the neighborhood street lights did little more than silhouetted him against the glass. His slumped shoulders and head hanging dejectedly told Frank all he needed to know.

"Ham, are you hungry? Can we go fix a sandwich? As long as it's not a BLT I mean."

Frank's effort at humor fell on deaf ears and Ham mumbled, "Thanks, I'm not hungry."

"Look buddy, you may still be in a wheelchair, but how many 13-year-olds can punch somebody from across the room? Or make things fly around at will? You've still got your super powers and I think they're permanent; unlike angel possession which is temporary."

"I'm not upset because an angel can't fix me. I've already settled into this role and I'm comfortable with it," Ham replied dejectedly.

"Then what on earth is going on?" Frank asked brusquely. "Are you pouting because you didn't get to go fight the bad guys? Because let me tell you there's plenty of them right outside and with all the angels gone, we're going to need your help more than ever."

"No, it's not that either. I'm looking forward to kicking some bad guy butt," Ham replied now in a monotone.

"Then tell me; what's the matter with you please?" Frank asked gently.

"Priscilla isn't going to want anything to do with me now that she can walk and all again," he admitted.

"What?" Frank shouted. "Is that what you're moping around about? Boy, have you got it all wrong," he shouted joyfully.

"What are you so happy about and what do you mean?" Ham shouted back.

"What's all the shouting about?" Clara called from the doorway.

"This bonehead thinks Pris isn't going to want anything to do with him now that she's not in a wheelchair anymore," Frank said with exasperation.

"Dear, he's not a bonehead any more than you are," Clara chided gently. "Although he is wrong in his conclusion," she continued, rolling across the room to stop at Ham's side.

"Priscilla would still want to be with you if she could fly and you were totally bedridden," Clara offered, using the most understandable analogy she could come up with.

"How do either of you know that?" Ham asked. "Oh yeah, you're clairvoyant."

"I don't need to be clairvoyant to know that Ham," she replied. "All I have to do is look at her when you're in the room. She's got it bad for you, young man."

"I'm glad you can tell because I sure don't see it," Ham quipped.

"Because she looks at you the way I still look at Frank," Clara said sweetly, looking up at her startled husband.

Ham looked up beseechingly at Frank for confirmation who gave him a befuddled shrug. "How am I supposed to understand females?" he said. "I'm just a cop."

Ham hung his head one more time and whispered softly, "I'm sorry God."

And for the second time in one evening, in one household, God spoke to one of his children.

"No need to apologize little one, I knew you would figure it out soon enough."

"But why didn't You just tell me?" Ham asked plaintively.

"You needed to hear it from one of your own kind."

"Okay, so I get to keep my super powers?" Ham asked, getting excited.

"Absolutely and you're going to need them in about 20 seconds."

"Huh?" Ham said. Turning to Frank he said, "God told me I get to keep my super powers and I'd need them in about 20 seconds."

There was an explosion from the front of the house and they all clearly heard the front door smash against the wall as it was blown open.

"I wish they'd quit doing that," Frank said.

TWENTY-THREE

FRANK WAS FIRST TO the entrance of the room, weapon at high ready. Ham was ten seconds behind him but it was a long ten seconds. Frank spotted four men who must have felt the house was empty because they were standing in a loose circle discussing their options in low tones.

As Frank listened, a middle-aged man with long, stringy red hair and horrible acne scars on his face and neck spoke. "He said to bring him the kid in the wheelchair and the hospital says he's been discharged."

"I know that numb-nuts, but you also said he'd be here or at his dad's place. He wasn't there and he's not here. So what next genius?" said a large man with a gravel voice.

"If we go back without him, he's not going to be happy," observed a slightly overweight but otherwise pretty young girl who looked like she might be a teenager.

All four individuals were carrying long guns. Scarface had an AR platform and the pretty girl had a lever-action western rifle. But what brought Frank up short was the weapon Gravel Voice carried. Hanging from his relaxed one-hand grip was a Sentinel Arms Striker 12 otherwise known as a Street Sweeper. This particular shotgun had a 12 round drum magazine and 18 inch barrel; it was strictly an anti-personnel device.

"Why don't you imbeciles all shut up and let me think?" barked the fourth man.

Obviously in charge, this man radiated menace. When he spoke the other three averted their gaze to the floor and took on a beaten posture. This man held a riot gun loosely in his left hand.

The sound of Ham's chair became audible to all four intruders simultaneously and Frank had just decided he needed to take out the big man first even if he wasn't the leader, but only if they refused to surrender. With four of them against him and a five-shot revolver he felt doubtful about that scenario.

"The kid must be here," said Scarface.

"Idiot, the wife is in a chair as well," replied the big man.

All four had begun to raise their weapon to a ready position as they turned toward the rear of the house; Frank knew his time was up. Stepping partially behind the cover of the alcove wall he raised his pistol to point directly at the big man.

"Police, weapons on the floor, now," he commanded.

Big man grabbed the fore grip of the shotgun and raised the business end toward Frank. A single round from Frank's 357 Magnum penetrated the man's shirtfront and snapped away the second button on his polo shirt. The big man took one stumbling step backward, still trying to raise his weapon.

Frank's attention had already turned to the leader but Scarface was frighteningly fast. He triggered the AR weapon even as it was still rising and it barked a staccato line of bullet gouges across the wood floor in Frank's direction. Frank had time to throw one diving shot at the man as he fell behind the wall.

He knew the sheetrock wouldn't even slow down a rifle bullet at this distance, especially from a weapon capable of fully-automatic fire. Out of the periphery of his vision as he fell he saw Scarface twist to his right and heard him cry out. *Tagged you, bastard*, Frank thought as he considered his next move.

Beginning at head height a line of explosion erupted above Frank and began to descend in foot-long gaps. Each was accompanied by the explosion of a shotgun blast from the riot gun. Frank duck-walked around the alcove wall into the kitchen, intent on flanking the remaining two or three.

As he neared the edge of the wall from the kitchen into the living room the bark of a large-caliber rifle added to the cacophony in the house and one of the cabinet doors in the kitchen exploded into fragments. The impact point was directly in line with where Frank's head would have been had he peeked around the corner.

Someone knew what they were doing. They were trying to box him in, knowing they could continue to blast holes through the short wall until they eventually got lucky and hit him. Even a grazing hit from the high-powered rifle round or the obvious slugs coming out of the riot gun would take him out long enough for them to finish him off.

Ham had arrived at the hallway entrance to the living room and before Frank could react, he turned into the room.

"No," was all Frank could shout as he dove into the living room from his side of the wall. He was desperate to draw their attention from the unarmed youth in the wheelchair. Frank had simply forgotten Ham's abilities and as he brought his revolver in line with the leader's torso, Ham flicked his hand at the girl with the rifle and she vanished.

The leader had brought his shotgun to bear on Ham just as Frank fired. The heavy pistol bullet struck the leader just behind his right ear, exploding a fist-sized chunk of his skull against the living room wall. The leader collapsed like a marionette whose strings had been cut.

Scarface was struggling to bring himself into a sitting position against the wall next to the front door. He had no thought for his weapon; he was too busy trying to breathe. Frank's bullet had torn through his right upper torso, nicking the Subclavian artery as it passed through the top of his lung, which was now filling up with his own blood.

"Help me," Scarface whispered through bubbling, bloody froth.

"Who is *he* that sent you here and why does he want Ham?" Frank asked dispassionately. A little voice in his head was saying *you need to call for a bus* but he was ignoring it.

"I'm dying," said the red-haired man, sweat pouring from his face as his body went into shock.

"Tell me who sent you and I'll call an ambulance," Frank repeated calmly.

Ham rolled up next to the drowning man and, as Scarface's eyes rolled back in his head, he placed his good hand on the man's uninjured shoulder.

"Begone," he spoke softly and Frank thought he was sending him away.

As Frank began to object the man convulsed and a dark flash of power emanated from him. The man's composure changed and he sighed gently, as if pleased. Then his head rolled to the side and his body convulsed once more as his death rattle escaped his bloody lips.

Removing his hand, Ham said, "I forced the demon out of his body and back into the Pit before he died so his soul might have a chance at redemption," Ham said reverently. "God showed me how after I promised to save as many human souls as I could in the coming apocalypse."

Tears were coursing down his cheeks, and he looked at Frank with wonder. "God loves us and He wants us to succeed. But He says if we fail it's the end of the world as we know it. He says His prophet John was very accurate in his description."

Clara rolled into the room looking at Frank, Ham, and the carnage of her home. "We'll need to find another home when this is all over," she said sadly. "I'll never be able to sleep in this house again." Turning to her husband she smiled, and her eyes flashed brilliant white.

"You're such a good and faithful man Frank Kratos, and my Father is very pleased with you," Raquel praised.

"How can that be when I've just killed three men?" Frank asked in awe. "Doesn't that violate one of his commandments?"

"Those men had given their souls to Lucifer and are lost by their own hands. And my Father said *thou shalt not murder*. Mankind has twisted that along with much of his guidance to suit their own peculiar needs." Raquel answered. "But my Father has instructed this new young prophet on the manner by which he might turn the tide of the battle. We must hasten to Hell's Gate without delay."

"I'll have to get Clara settled somewhere, so there's no way you can go with us," Frank rejoined. "Because there's absolutely no way I can or will allow her in the path of danger."

Light flared in Clara's eyes and Raquel smiled. "Even with an Archangel in residence?"

Frank looked dubiously at Raquel and then acquiesced.

"Let me talk to Clara please," he replied. The light faded from her eyes and Clara looked lovingly into her husband's.

"My darling, I have seen a glimpse of what news Raquel brings back from her visits to her world, and the images God is sending with her are horrific. It is unbearable for me to consider not helping if anything I can do will change that outcome."

Turning at Ham she continued. "In this current future the entire world is enslaved by demons riding human forms and they treat mankind with contempt and utter cruelty. They murder and rape in wanton fashion and much of their progeny are demon-spawned. Within a generation the planet becomes a dark pit of despair similar to where they have been for eons, which seems so wrong. If they wanted out of their despair, why bring it here with them?"

Tears welled on the cusp of her trembling lids and Clara returned her gaze to Frank. "We must do anything, everything, to prevent this. No sacrifice is too great to save mankind." The tears escaped her eyes and coursed unchecked down her pale cheeks.

"What are you doing now?" she asked.

Frank was searching through the pockets of the four dead assailants scattered around his living room. As he took various types of ammunition off their still forms he said, "I'm gathering their weapons. I have a feeling we're going to need all the firepower we can muster."

TWENTY-FOUR

CLARA, HAM, AND FRANK arrived in Lubbock just after 4:30 am. As in Marrisa's van, Ham had found sufficient tie-down points to secure his chair in the back. Frank was using his hand-held radio, now that they were in range of Sariel/Jason and the police walkie-talkie he still carried.

"Jason, we're on highway 62 about to cross highway 289, how far out are we?" he asked.

"You're about 20 minutes, Lieutenant and you're cutting it close. There's been a lot of activity at the trestle," Jason replied with a touch of panic in his voice. "Take 62 to MLK, it's about two miles. Go south a quarter mile to Canyon Lake Drive *after* the bridge. It's a loop so there are two turn-offs, take the *second* one. We have people set up halfway down the first one. Follow it about a mile and a half to the dam. It's the best place for Ham and Clara to be overwatch."

"That adds up to four miles, how is that twenty minutes?" Frank grilled.

"Canyon Lake Drive is a winding two-lane and it's residential. There's not much traffic at 4:30, but you wouldn't want to try straightening the curves in your van, I don't think," Jason replied. The panic in his voice was nearing hysteria and Frank was concerned for his reliability.

"I'll be careful," Frank assured him. "You might want to take a few deep breaths, Jason. You're sounding a little frazzled."

When there was no reply, Frank raised the radio to his mouth to speak again but Jason's voice came out of the walkie. Only this time, it was calm and sounded different; angel different. "Jason has agreed I should take over for now," Camael said. "The things he's seeing are difficult for him to comprehend."

"We'll be there in ten minutes," Frank assured him. "What should we expect and what do you need us to do?"

"Demons have been streaming through the gate since moments after we arrived at the old railroad bridge," Camael said. "We have been able to hold them back for the most part and those who have slipped past must contend with

Hemah and Arariel on the road. We have a moment's respite as they gather on the other side for another assault. I have yet to determine how they managed to breach the gate initially, but that consideration is now mute."

"Moot," Frank heard Marrisa say in the background. "The issue is moot. Mute means you can't speak."

"The first we encountered were humans with demon riders and we dispatched them easily enough," Camael continued. "Azrael and I are considering the possibility that those humans might have performed a ritual which weakened the portal sufficiently for the others to come through. Once that happened their combined powers were sufficient to open it completely."

"Have they heard from Cassiel and Ariel on how many they've stopped?" Raquel asked.

When Frank relayed the question, Marrisa answered. "Camael is busy with some new arrivals so asked me to continue the conversation. Cassiel told Azrael, so of course I overheard, that they've stopped a dozen or more pure demons searching for hosts. Ariel and Camael think more than that have gotten past us."

"Between them and Adriel they've stopped at least fifty demons right here at the gate. Adriel is really scary you know. She just touches a demon and they burst into flames," she finished. "She's the angel of Death but what a way to go, even for a demon."

"So is she saying there may be some demons coming around our side of the loop?" Ham asked, quickly analyzing the scenario.

Frank nodded, raising the radio to relay their thoughts as two nightmare figures leaped out into the road in front of the van. Frank instinctively jammed on the brakes and cut the wheel. The ABS caused the front tires to skitter on the asphalt as the vehicle slewed clockwise. One of the creatures resembled a man's torso with the head of a bull and the legs of a lion. Its arms were heavily hairy but human until the end where they terminated in three razor-sharp claws.

The second creature wasn't remotely humanoid; it had eight tentacles writhing from the foremost end of a quadruped body which might have been a bull or maybe a horse. But the legs were thick and powerful like those on an elephant.

Frank was frozen in abject terror. Raquel spoke words of power and thrust her hands in front of her face at the charging juggernaut. The creature faltered in mid-stride before regaining its footing and continuing its charge.

Raquel screamed a similar phrase and the thump felt inside the van must have been nothing compared to the detonation outside. The body exploded in front of the windshield, showering the glass with thick, viscous orange goo and gobs of blackened flesh. Overpowering odors of sulphur and rotting meat permeated the air and Ham struggled to check his rising gorge.

Ham had watched over Frank's shoulder as the man-thing had charged the driver's window and now thrust his hand out in a clenching motion, twisting his hand as if trying to open a doorknob. The man-thing reached for Frank's window and froze, arms extended out in front of the torso. It vibrated and bounced as if a volcano were preparing to go off inside it, blurring the image of the creature as if seen through a wad of cellophane. Then it vanished with an audible pop.

"Yes!" Ham exclaimed. "God told me to lay waste to the demons of the Pit, and I am," he shouted.

Raquel turned in Clara's wheelchair and gazed at Ham. "My Father has given you immense power for a mortal, Ham. Use it wisely."

Frank shook himself before restarting the van and putting it in gear. "I seriously need a drink," he muttered under his breath. "There's a housing subdivision to our right and the lake to our left, so I'm assuming they're trying to get to people in hopes of finding a host?"

Raquel nodded. "We must get closer to the gate to best stop them before they can reach humans."

As they approached the curve leading to the dam crossroad, three more unusual apparitions appeared in the roadway; two straight out of Dante's inferno. They looked a lot like goblins created by Hollywood while the third was a beautiful woman dressed in a diaphanous gown. This time Frank didn't hesitate, flooring the van and aiming it at all three.

The woman seemed to become transparent while the two goblins impacted the front of the van at 30 miles per hour and began scrambling up the grill toward the windshield. As they grabbed the wipers for a handhold Frank switched the wiper motor on and flung both creatures off into the night. Jamming the brakes, he spun the van 180 degrees and pointed the headlights at the three figures.

One of the goblins had struck a tree and was scrabbling about as if its back was broken. The other was regaining its feet and looked ready to charge the van again. Frank rolled his window down and thrust his revolver out, firing twice at the goblin on the ground. It jerked once and stilled, so Frank changed his aim and fired twice more at the other.

It leapt aside impossibly quickly and all three occupants of the van saw the bullets spark orange trails across the asphalt. As the goblin leapt for the van Ham repeated his clenching and twisting motion. The goblin vibrated in mid-air and vanished.

Raquel had been moving her hands and arms in a complicated pattern in front of her face as all this was happening and now thrust both hands away from her as if throwing something. The apparition wavered, becoming transparent again before beginning to change shape and color.

It transitioned from stark white to yellow and then orange. The image became even more tenuous as it changed to bright red. A piercing wail cut the night air like some mournful locomotive whistle heard across the silence of the vast southwestern plains. Then the spirit, ghost, or whatever it was shrank down to a finite point and popped out of existence.

"That was a wraith and I had no idea they had joined forces with the demons," Raquel explained. "Although they exist in a plane separate from the Pit they can move between dimensions much more readily than my Brothers and Sisters. They are generally harmless, more inquisitive than anything else, but I sensed a malevolent cause in this one."

"I was confirmed when it attempted to drag me back across the curtain to its side." Raquel paused, shaking her head in a very real display of human confusion. "This is indeed a new condition all the protectors must be made aware of immediately. If they are caught unprepared a wraith can strip them from their vessel, leaving it unprotected."

Frank keyed the radio and passed Raquel's observation on to the others. "How do we inform the pair on the other side of the lake road?" Frank asked.

"I'll be right back," Raquel said, and the brilliance in Clara's eyes vanished.

"Well that was certainly interesting," Clara said with a notable quiver in her voice. "Raquel barely got ahead of the wraith's power. It had already connected with her energy and was sucking her out of me. Raquel says I helped her remain by flowing positive thoughts to her. At least I know I can help in some small way."

Then her eyes flared white and Raquel was back. "We must advance onto the dam so Ham has a clear view of the Gate where it opens at the end of the old train bridge," she directed.

Frank put the van in gear once more and rolled slowly along the dam road until Raquel spoke. "Stop here and turn the headlights to the south." The headlights exposed nothing but treetops and open ground.

"I can sense the Gate is directly in front of us but Ham must be able to see it in order to take action." Both Frank and Ham could feel the frustration and anxiety emanating from Raquel. Her Brothers were in danger and she had the key to lock the Gate, but how to use it?

"Hang on," Ham blurted. "I thought I saw a dirt road back that way a little."

"I'm not going off-road in this van with you two in it," Frank stated. "No discussion; it's not happening."

"Let me check out the map app on my phone," Ham said. He worked his hand across the screen of the smart phone until he had the map he wanted. "I was right. The dirt road leads around a line of trees to the end of the bridge," he said, handing the phone to Frank. Turning to Raquel he asked, "Where is the Gate in reference to the bridge?"

Clara was looking at the phone in Frank's hand, trying to see the map as well. When he held it out for her to view she brightened considerably. "As best as I can tell, this end of the bridge *is* the Gate. Adriel and Azrael are standing on either side while Camael stands ready for all who exit. Frank, that dirt road leads to within a safe yet visible distance of the Gate. Once he can see it Ham can close it."

"I can?" Ham asked, amazed. "I heard you say that before but thought I misunderstood. How can I close the Gate?"

"If my Father has given you power to wield souls and vanquish demons, then you are his chosen prophet for this age and can do anything you need to defeat the hordes," Raquel said as if quoting.

"So I can do more than make demons disappear?" Ham asked, now excited.

"Ham, I daresay you could make *me* disappear," Raquel said solemnly.

"Now why would I want to do that?" Ham blurted.

"Not that you would or should Ham, only that you are capable," she replied.

"Frank, take us down the dirt road only until I can see the Gate," he said.

"There has to be another way," Frank argued. "I know Clara is protected by your presence Raquel, but I just learned that wraiths are real and can pull you from her body. And Ham has no protection of any kind."

"Did you not just hear what she said Frank?" Ham seethed. "I can do anything I need to stop these demons and close the Gate. Now take me down the road or I'll go by myself," he said, already reaching for the tie-down strap releases.

"Just wait a damn minute," Frank bellowed. The other two were startled at his outburst. "This is all moving too fast for me. Will you give me one minute to think?" he exclaimed in exasperation.

Ham sat mute, as did Raquel. Frank looked at them expectantly but Ham only said, "Fifty seconds."

"Oh for crying out loud," Frank groused, opening his door and walking around to the rear of the van. When he opened the rear doors Ham released one of the three straps holding him in place and was reaching for another when Frank spoke. "Just tighten that right back up, mister. You're not going anywhere."

As he spoke, he pulled a panel off the inside wall of the van and removed an AR rifle along with two large-capacity magazines and a semi-automatic handgun. "Ever fire one of these before?" he asked, holding it out for Ham to see.

Ham mutely shook his head so Frank thrust the pistol in the back of his waistband. Slapping a magazine into the rifle, he pulled the charging handle and allowed it to snap back into place. "I just want more firepower than my revolver," he offered by way of explanation.

Entering the driver's door he propped the rifle against the front doorframe and sat the buttplate in the step well. Removing his revolver from the shoulder holster he pulled a speed loader from his jacket pocket and, ejecting the cylinder onto the doghouse over the engine, reloaded.

Sliding the revolver back into its holster he reached behind his back and pulled the pistol out, press checking it to see that a round was in the chamber. He wedged this barrel first into the space between the seat and armrest of the captain's chair he sat in. "Now I'm ready. Where's this dirt road?"

TWENTY-FIVE

"IT SHOULDN'T BE MORE than about 200 yards according to the map," Ham offered.

Raquel was craning her neck to see further up the road and Ham couldn't see anything with her on one side and Frank in the driver's seat. The dirt road made a slow sweep to the left and their headlights illuminated the old train bridge, but there was no one in sight.

"Pull the front to the right so that the rear doors face the bridge," Raquel directed.

Once positioned, Frank got out and opened those doors. Ham had already turned his chair around in the tight confines of the van and sat facing Frank when the doors opened.

"I'm not sure what I'm supposed to do here," Ham said cautiously.

"You are the Prophet of the Father," Raquel said regally. "You have the power to close the gate."

"But there's no gate here," Ham responded plaintively.

As if in rebuttal to his claim the night began to shimmer near the west end of the bridge. Angry red and yellow sparks flew from seemingly nowhere about four feet off the ground. A bright orange glow like the rising sun filled the center of the space.

Frank had turned to watch the display and Ham heard Raquel turning Clara's chair around in the center of the van. A figure emerged from the shadows of the woods to their left and Frank's revolver was instantly pointed at it. Ham had raised his hand to throw power at whatever it was when the figure called out.

"Easy, LT, it's me; Omikawa," Jason said.

"That's the second time tonight I've almost put a bullet in you," Frank growled.

"Well I'm pretty sure a bullet won't do me much harm right now," Jason quipped.

Then his eyes flared and Camael spoke to Raquel. "It is good you are here Sister. Amom's horde amasses on the opposite side and I fear we will not contain them without your help."

Turning to Ham, he continued. "Prophet, you must focus all your energies on closing that portal," he commanded. An expanding ball of coruscating fire and light was now beginning to fission the night sky.

"But I don't know how," Ham said again, sounding both frustrated and frightened.

"Be not afraid Prophet, I will guide you, as will Sister."

Raquel had moved Clara's chair up to where she was directly behind Ham. She reached and placed her hand on his shoulder and Ham felt soothing calm flow through his being. Moving to the open van doors Camael reached for Ham as Frank stepped around the van toward the driver's door.

"Open yourself to our power as you did before when you resurrected Frank," Raquel instructed.

Ham had just a moment to think *resurrected?* Then he felt Camael in his mind as he had Uriel in the hospital. *Focus with us on the gate and reversing the power being used to tear open space*, he heard Camael say in his head. Following their lead Ham stared intently at the roiling wall of power even as it continued to grow and coalesce. He could sense energy rising from deep inside him but was uncertain how to control or direct it.

"Just like when you move people from one location to another, move the power of the gate back to whence it came," Raquel said softly in his ear.

Redoubling his effort of will, Ham pushed against the force he could feel emanating from the gate and felt something yield. Encouraged, he began to push harder, focusing his mind on that single point of resistance.

"It's working," he exclaimed, elatedly. He could see the gate begin to shrink and felt it's presence diminishing.

A sharp report sounded from the front of the van and Raquel's hand slumped from Ham's shoulder. Immediately the gate began to expand rapidly and Ham felt himself losing control of the force within him.

"Clara, no!" Frank bellowed.

Unable to turn, his concentration completely broken, Ham lost his mental grip on his new-found power.

Camael gripped his forearm more firmly and ground out, "We must continue to resist the force of the portal."

Ham's mind was scattered. "What happened to Clara?" he asked over his shoulder.

A staccato burst of weapons fire answered his question as he heard Frank cursing like he had never witnessed before.

"Come and get some, you bastards," Frank screamed.

Camael pulled on Ham's arm to get his attention but Ham yanked free. "My sister is healing Clara as we speak but her wound is grievous," Camael explained.

"What wound?" Ham demanded.

"A human in the woods beyond shot her," he said pointing toward the front of the van.

"How bad is it?" Ham insisted.

"They blew her brains out, that's how bad it is," Frank yelled. "Over hear, shit-bird," he screamed as the rapid repeat of his rifle claimed another aggressor. "Jason I could use your help up here, there's gotta be at least 30 of them," he barked. The clatter of the magazine being replaced added counterpoint to his desperate plea.

Camael gazed deeply into Ham eyes for a moment before he spoke. "You do not need our assistance to close the gate," he said. "I can feel the level of power within you; you are indeed the most substantial of Father's Prophets I have ever witnessed." He was shaking his head in awe. "I do not understand how your frail human mind can even tolerate such energy. You must do what needs be done."

The light in his eyes extinguished, and Jason Omikawa called out, "On my way LT."

Moments later Ham heard the boom of the riot gun as Jason opened up on their attackers. Ham exulted in the confidence Camael had displayed and turned again to the gate. He could see Marrisa standing beside it along with Daniel, the Navy Seal.

"Daniel," Ham called. "Wouldn't you be better in a firefight? That way Camael can help Marrisa stop whoever comes through. He is the Archangel, after all."

Immediately both figures turned from where they were and raced past each other to their new assignments.

"There's a bunch of weapons back here," Ham called as Daniel drew near. The Seal stopped just long enough to gather up several of the weapons lying on the floor of the van, grinning at Ham.

"Good call kid," he said as he rounded the corner of the van and entered into the fray.

"Frank, I'm going to flank this group in the woods to our left and get them in an "L" ambush line," Daniel told Frank. "There may be only two of us but with this baby, I bet it'll work," he said, hefting the Street Sweeper Frank had brought from the assault on his home.

"Go to it, I'll lay down cover fire," Frank responded, slapping a new magazine into his rifle and pulling the pistol from under the armrest to lay it in the seat beside him.

Daniel sprinted away and Frank marveled at how fast even a Navy Seal could run when they had an angel power booster. Four figures burst from the tree line headed straight for the van. An apparent suicide mission, it spoke to how desperately the demons in control wanted the gate opened. Frank judiciously held his fire until they were committed from cover before he began ruthlessly cutting them down. They fired as they ran so their aim was poor.

Even still, numerous rounds impacted the front of the van. One shattered the driver's window showering Frank with nuggets of safety glass. All four figures were dropped and still before they were within 30 feet of the van.

A second group of six emerged running from the trees. They were angling toward the other side of the van to keep it between them and Frank. The booming report from the street sweeper dropped them all within yards of the tree line as Daniel opened up in a crossfire.

No additional groups came into the open but now slugs began tearing through the windshield and ricocheting off the metal door frame. Frank pulled back to reload yet again as a huge hole appeared in the door panel where he had just stood. A thunderous roar followed it instantly. Glancing up, he saw a large man at the edge of the woods leaning against a tree with an incredibly long rifle held to his shoulder. It boomed like a cannon and another gaping hole cored through the windshield and the side of the van above his head.

"Ham, Clara, get down," he screamed. "Get to some kind of cover, behind a tire or away from the van. He's got a BMG."

Another eight-inch hole burst from the side of the van next to Frank's face, spraying him with shards of sheet metal. One two inch sliver struck Frank at the outer corner of his eye, penetrating the orb and lodging in his left nostril. He screamed as he clutched his face but had enough presence of mind to not touch the sharp metal. An answering scream came from the man at the tree and Frank looked up expecting to see him charging across the field of fire. Instead Frank saw the rifle laying on the ground and the man clutching his own head.

"Frank, come to me," Ham called.

Frank made his way to the back of the van and Ham reached for him. "I'm sorry I couldn't stop him sooner, I was focused on the gate. Move your hand so I can fix your eye."

Frank looked stupefied with his remaining eye but did as his young charge directed. Ham placed his palm over Frank's ravaged eye and closed his own eyes for only a few seconds. When he pulled his hand away, Frank was whole.

"How...?" Frank began but Ham cut him off with a motion.

"No time," he replied. "Go stop them so I can get this God-cursed gate closed."

Frank moved back to the front of the van but glanced back through the open interior. Ham had his good arm raised above his head, almost touching the roof of the vehicle. His hair stood straight out as if he were about to be struck by lightning and a pulsing violet orb surrounded his body. As Frank looked on, frozen in amazement, the orb darkened to deep purple and golden flashes began to course through it. Another bullet glanced off the shattered windshield at an odd angle and went whining into the dark.

Frank grabbed up the pistol from the seat and began rapid-firing at the figure kneeling directly in front of the van. He was less than twenty feet away and right out in the open but his intent was hitting Ham. The man saw Frank move back to the driver's door and turned toward him.

Three slugs from Frank's pistol struck the man in the torso. The lever-action rifle in his hands barked once more and the bullet struck Frank squarely in the chest. Clutching his heart, Frank staggered backward two steps before falling lifelessly onto his side.

TWENTY-SIX

"YOU SHALL NOT PASS," Camael called from Jason's body as he wielded a flaming sword of light against the vile throng.

A deluge of misshapen creatures were squirming through the partially open gate as it hung in the air at the end of the old train bridge. Even as they hit the ground and began to run they met their end. When the edge of Camael's sword or Adriel's hand touched them they were flashed into fire and returned to the Pit in flames. They were indeed a fearsome pair to behold yet now and again one of the horde slipped by; there were just so many of them.

"Come 'ere, ya little freak," came a call from behind them.

Neither of them turned but both heard the boom of the shotgun Hofniel wielded in Daniel's body. When the demons of the horde were slain by non-angelic power they apparently just dissolved into a small puddle of primordial ooze. *Who knew?*

"I can't catch them all," Adriel called as yet another slipped by.

"I'm running low on ammo," Hofniel called.

"We must not let them pass or all may be lost," Camael shouted as he beheaded a gruesome figure with an emaciated human form and two heads, neither of which had any skull above the nose.

"I knew we'd miss all the fun standing guard out on that lonely road," Hemah said as he walked up next to Hofniel brandishing a lethal-looking short-barreled shotgun.

"Brother, did you abandon your post?" Camael called incredulously, dispatching another nightmare creature back to the Pit.

"No, we were relieved by a local citizen's militia group, as they described themselves," Arariel answer. She held a crossbow of all things and had a quiver of bolts slung across her chest. "They arrived 10 minutes ago in time to witness Hemah slaughter three of the Pit's denizens. Once the initial shock of their appearance wore off the group assured us the demons would be just another opponent for them to vanquish."

"Those weren't their actual words," Hemah finished. "Their version was much more colorful. Some of the phrases even good Catholic Patrick laughed at."

"Well join in, there are ample numbers to keep us all busy," Camael ordered. "I'm going to check on Raquel."

Looking at Arariel he shook his head. "A crossbow?"

"Hey, it was offered and reminded me of my time in the Han dynasty," she smirked.

As he approached the open rear doors of the van, Camael noted two things. One was the figure of his sister once again holding her hand to Ham's shoulder and the deepening hue of the energy sphere which he knew meant the gate would soon be gone. The second thing was the still shape of Frank Kratos on the ground with Hofniel kneeling beside him.

No one within the van had apparently witnessed his death and Hofniel knew not to distract them even though it broke his heart. He knew the longer Frank's body was without life the harder it would be to help him recover and the less complete it would be. Rushing to his side, Camael and Jason were having an argument inside Jason's skull.

"You've done it before with Marrisa," Jason was yelling.

"Agreed and Father was less than pleased. I do not wish to incur His wrath again for the same transgression," Camael replied.

"Let me speak to Daniel," Jason insisted.

"Hofniel is not an Archangel, he cannot resurrect the dead as we can," Camael replied.

"If you don't do something I will reject you from my body and inform Raquel," Jason countered. "She's been close enough to Frank for long enough she won't hesitate to save him."

"That won't be necessary," Raquel said from Clara's body as her wheelchair rounded the front of the van. "All the psychic energy flying around out here is as bad as the testosterone level at a bar fight on Friday night."

The chair stopped and Clara jerked her head up as she burst into racking sobs at the sight of her dead husband. For long moments nothing happened. Then slowly, the ragged hole in Frank's back from the passage of the bullet began to close. No scar formed and no writhing of tissue occurred; the wound just diminished until it vanished. Frank thrashed once on the ground before leaping to his feet. As soon as he was upright, Clara's eyes flashed white and Raquel was back in her long-term host.

"How shall we reconcile this unwarranted occupancy of this host with Father?" Camael asked sadly.

"No need for grief my friend," Frank said as he walked over to Camael and laid a hand on his forearm. "I gave Raquel permission to occupy my body several days ago. I was concerned something might happen to me while Clara and Ham were with me at our house. I didn't want them to be defenseless so Raquel and I came to an agreement."

"And Father agrees with this?" Camael asked dubiously.

"Father has given me great latitude with Clara and Frank. They are both destined to be part of saving this planet and its residents," Raquel replied.

Her tone was solemn but there was a twinkle of mirth in her voice. Apparently she enjoyed teasing her brother.

"What about the gate?" Frank blurted suddenly.

In the midst of dying and being resurrected for the second time in 24 hours, he had temporarily forgotten their mission. All heads turned toward the back of the van and were met with an indescribable sight. Dozens of demons in all manner of sizes, shapes, and horrors were suspended in acts of running. Some were in mid-stride while others were leaping for their nemeses awaiting them on Earth's side of the gate. Arariel, Azrael, and Hemah were all frozen in martial poses, preparing to attack whatever despicable resident of the Pit was nearest.

"I don't know how much longer I can hold them," Ham panted. Sweat was pouring down his face and his raised arm trembled and shook.

Camael rushed to his side and Raquel rolled around to the side door hydraulic ramp to reenter the van. Supporting his arm Camael asked, "What is it you've done? Why have you chosen to suspend them rather than close the gate? Surely if you have this much authority to freeze time you can close the rift."

"I was closing it when something more powerful than I've ever felt began pushing through," Ham explained. Camael had clambered into the van and placed his hands on Ham's back and under his forearm, helping him hold his hand aloft. "Raquel had to save Frank so I told her I'd hold the line for as long as needed. You were right; I *can* close it by myself. It almost *was* closed when *something* started pushing back from the other side."

"Release the time hold and let us end this permanently," Camael ordered.

"Give it one more minute while we get reloaded," Frank said, reaching for his last magazine and pressing a fresh one into the pistol.

"I'm all out," Hofniel said, rattling his shotgun.

"There's a box of 25 slugs under the seat," Frank said, turning toward the driver's door.

Ham uttered a single explosive sound and recoiled from the direction of the gate. All action started again and Frank yelled, "We aren't ready."

"I didn't let go, something yanked time out of my hands," Ham gasped. "It felt like I was being electrocuted."

Arariel and Hemah resumed their fight while Adriel reached for the next demon squirming through the hole. Suddenly Azrael flew backward in a high arc landing with a thud 30 feet away, flat on her back. Everyone heard the whoosh as the air was forced from her lungs.

"Cease your efforts Ham," Camael said. "I know who this is."

Stepping from the back of the van, Camael strode toward the center of the rift. As he neared it a massive, darkly-writhing, winged creature of such foul appearance as to defy description emerged from the hole. It was like watching a baby being born, only this womb was the eternal Pit of Hell and the baby was one of the ruling Princes.

"Amom, you are not welcome here," Camael called even as the figure burst through the stretching portal.

"Brother, the residents of this pitiful planet have called us forth from the netherworld and we have as much right to their vessels as do you to yours," Amom replied.

The voice which came from the figure sounded like a deep-voiced announcer speaking from the bottom of a well with the bass turned all the way up on the amplifier. The walls of the van vibrated with the intensity of it.

"I see no vessels for you to occupy brother," Camael replied slightly.

"Our vessels await us in the world and we shall go to them *now*," Amom bellowed.

Ham noted the Archdemon carried a long, twisted shaft which resembled a great oak tree branch. Looking closer he could see the images of many faces twisted in agony, etched along its length. As he watched, the mouths on the faces moved and wordless cries issued forth. Galvanized by the thought of all those souls in torment, Ham turned his chair around and told Clara to get out so he could as well.

Amom swung his staff like a club, one-handed, toward everything in his path. Demon, angel, or human; it didn't matter. Hemah and Arariel were cast aside like matchsticks and dozens of scampering demons were crushed by the speed and weight of the blow.

Camael's sword appeared in his hands and he swung it two-handed to meet Amom's staff. The impact from their meeting deafened everything with the ability to hear. The concussion was so great it turned Clara's chair on its side where she had just rolled off the lift. Clara was thrown from the chair sprawling sideways onto the hard-packed dirt.

The blow stalled Amom in his tracks. He recoiled slightly, catching himself before he toppled.

Standing tall and flapping his wings for effect he said laughingly, "Is that the best you've got, little Brother?" and he swung again.

This time his staff was used as a hammer, trying to drive Camael into the ground. Camael danced aside easily and he leapt across the brief distance between the two Archangels; one fallen, and one full of God's grace. His sword flashed and Amom's bellow sounded like the great noises Blue Whales make. A line of bright white scored its way down Amom's chest and thick, black, oozing fluid bubbled to the surface of the wound.

Stepping to his right Amom shrugged the wound off, even as it began to close and mend. "If that little scratch is all you have you may as well vacate now," he gloated. "I'm sure I can find one of my chief demons to ride that young morsel until we're ready to eat him."

Swinging the staff over his head, Amom stepped forward and delivered a crushing blow to the top of the van. Ham had just rolled off the lift and turned toward the fight. The concussion from the blow rattled him and caused his chair to rock. He hurtled forward to right it and slid to a halt at the back doors.

"So here is the puny mortal Father has deemed to be the savior of this weak and useless ball of mud," Amom sneered. "Let us see what strength Father thinks to have given you." Amom thrust his hand forward, palm out.

Ham sensed what was coming and threw his own force in return. The two balls of red and violet energy met mid-air and tangled together, roiling around in the night like a spasming, pulsating, light show tornado. In seconds the opposing powers detonated, pushing a shock wave out in all directions. Any remaining demons were cast as leaves before a maelstrom and it was good none of the angel's vessels had risen to their feet as of yet. The crushed van flipped end over front before rolling onto its side.

Frank stood where the van had been moments before. Utter disbelief shown on his face at his first sight of the behemoth. Hofniel stood beside him, shotgun hanging uselessly at his side.

"So bullets won't hurt this one?" Frank asked.

"I don't know, have you got an Elephant Gun, I believe Daniel calls it?" Hofniel replied.

Frank turned and sprinted for the tree line.

"At least one of your puny mortals sees the uselessness of your efforts and decides to run for its miserable life," Amom laughed.

Hofniel spied Clara lying on the ground struggling to sit up. He rushed to her side, righting her chair and lifting her back into it. "Thank you cousin," Raquel offered.

"My pleasure cousin," Hofniel replied.

"Amom, you have squandered your horde now and there are none left to join you in this ill-conceived effort," Camael called up to the giant. "Return to the pit before we are forced to vanquish you. I do not wish a rematch of the battle fought eons ago."

"So you *do* remember the thrashing I gave you?" Amom chortled. "Let me recall; was it from a blow such as *this*?" the Archdemon screamed, thrusting the tip of his staff at Camael who was standing well within striking range.

Camael's sword was quick in response to engage the side of the staff but not before the tip had struck a glancing blow off his shoulder. The strike spun him around and in the moment of imbalance, Amom struck again. Swatting at the struggling form of Camael, he meant to crush him.

"I shall smash you again just as I did so long ago," Amom sneered, grinning wickedly.

As the blow descended a roaring boom echoed across the opening and Amom cried out, grasping his shoulder and losing his grip on the staff. Already set in motion, the staff bounced off the hard earth and caromed off into the night. Removing his hand, Amom gazed in wonder at the hole in his shoulder.

From the edge of the trees Frank called out. "This puny human didn't run very far. *Say hello to my little friend*," he mimicked as he once again pulled the trigger on the Barrett 50 caliber. The round sped true to its target and a similar hole appeared in Amom's cheek at the edge of the lid below his right eye. "Sorry, sights are off a little. I was aiming for your forehead," Frank called tauntingly.

Bellowing his rage and pain while holding his hand over his injured eye, Amom took one long stride in Frank's direction where his outstretched leg met the blade of light in Camael's hands. This time it wasn't a slashing strike but more akin to chopping down a tree. The blade sunk deep into the front of Amom's leg, lodging in his shin. It stuck there and Camael was unable to retrieve it.

"I will skewer you with your own puny stick," Amom bellowed as he fell to one knee, yanking the blade from his leg. He screamed even louder as the wound opened further and fresh black vitriol began coursing down his leg. "Your efforts will not stop me from my vengeance Camael," he growled. "I shall vanquish all of you from this planet and then I will lay it to waste."

Raising the sword over his head, he turned toward Camael and felt yet another punch from Frank's rifle. This round penetrated his right ear and went straight into what should have been his brain. Clutching his head in both hands, dropping the sword, Amom screamed his agony and dropped to both knees. He roared in anger, pain, and frustration as he once again struggled to regain his footing.

"Your nuisance weapon will be the instrument of your death mortal," he roared. "I shall impale you upon it," and he lunged for Frank once again.

Deep purple force, pulsating and brilliant, slammed Amom back against the wall of the gate in waves. One of his arms disappeared through the hole and he quickly snatched it back, a different kind of pain written on his face. For the first time in their brief encounter, Amom looked uncertain. Drawing himself up, he addressed Ham.

"First things first; I must destroy you," he said calmly.

"Bring it," Ham called back fearlessly.

Amom dove across the forty foot opening, launching himself with arms outstretched to physically grab and crush the life from Ham. Midway in his leap a deep purple aura surrounded him and held him suspended in mid-air.

"You will *not* hurt my friends," Ham said, twisting his outstretched hand. Amom's scream of pain resounded into the night.

"You will *not* harm my *people*," Ham called again, whipping his wrist to one side. Amom's anguished cry filled the evening sky.

"And you will have *no more souls to torment*," Ham cried righteously. Pulling his arm into his chest, he punched it back out at the Archdemon.

A gargling cry escaped Amom's throat as he began to thrash and writhe about, suspended in his now darkening magenta prison. As the orb rolled around in the air dark fluid continued to spread inside. Flinging his arm away from his body, Ham pushed the prison up into the night sky. Higher and higher it soared, illuminated by the bright full moon. Amom could be seen thrashing about inside but the sphere continued to accelerate until it was finally out of sight.

"Where did you send him?" Raquel asked, rolling up next to Ham.

"I sensed if I sent him back to the Pit he would simply regain strength and followers, destined to try again," Ham explained. "I'm not sure he's going to find many followers on the Moon. " Ham paused at the faces all staring at him, mouths agape. "Hey I know I can't destroy him, so the next best thing is to neutralize his power, right?"

Glancing at the portal, Ham flicked his wrist and it popped out of existence. The night became suddenly much darker. Frank was pulling a flashlight from his jacket pocket to take account of what was left when a vehicle careened off the pavement, slewing about in the dirt before regaining control and heading toward the band of faithful warriors at break-neck speed.

"Get behind me," Ham called as all the angels formed a line in front of him. "Hey, if I can send an Archdemon to the moon I can stop a car," he complained.

"We cannot risk the Father's Prophet unless it is essential," Camael said matter-of-factly.

"In other words, we got this," Raquel smiled impishly.

The Hummer slewed sideways as the driver caught sight of the party in the headlights. The door flew open and a fully combat-armed man leapt from the front.

"Camael, there is trouble in Hellam Township. The fight does not go well there," the stranger said.

"Ah, Cassiel, how is it you have come this far so quickly?" Raquel asked.

"One of the party of defenders in PA, as they call it, had the phone number to the brotherhood group here in Texas. They were the ones who relieved Hemah and Arariel," Cassiel offered as if that explained everything.

"But how did you enter a vessel here if you were in *PA*?" Azrael asked, confused. "And is Priscilla alright?"

Turning to Azrael he said, "Your daughter is well Marrisa; Sariel takes good care of her."

Turning back to Raquel he said, "Apparently I can get permission to use a willing vessel over a *cell phone*?"

TWENTY-EIGHT

"THE GENERAL WISHES to speak with you all right away," the man announced.

"And just who is the General?" Frank asked, once again taking charge of the situation.

"Major General Hiram Martin, U.S. Marine Corps, retired; he's our CO," the man replied. Then as an afterthought, he extended his hand. "Forgive my lack of manners; Major Evan Jergenson, USMC, retired. Medically," he added, wiggling his right leg. A slight metallic clicking helped them all understand at least a portion of his right leg was artificial. "Most of the troops just call me Major J."

"Well Major J, you and I have about the same amount of authority with our rank here in Lubbock, Texas," Frank responded, smiling and accepting the proffered hand. "Which means none. I'm Lieutenant Franklin Kratos of the Chickasha, Oklahoma Police Department and a member of the Oklahoma Urban Task Force on Paranormal Activities. Most everyone calls me Frank except my troops, who just call me Lt."

When Frank announced the second part of his *Bona Fides*, everyone in the group turned to him in unison. Echoes of *huh?,...what?...* and *Frank?...* all jumbled together for a moment. Holding his hand up for silence, Frank addressed the information.

"There has been no need for any of you to be aware of that qualification, it makes no difference to our mission," he said casually. "Besides, Clara knew and I'm sure she shared it with Raquel."

Major J's eyes flared silver and Cassiel was back in the driver's seat. "I cannot overemphasize the imperative nature of our travelling to Hellam Township as quickly as possible."

"Well, just exactly *how* do you suggest we get there as quickly as possible?" Frank asked with an edge of frustration in his voice. "We can't just call someone there on the cell phone and jump bodies." Hesitating as he realized what he had just said, he started again. "Well, *most* of us can't; that is *I* can't, and..." that was when he realized he was the only person present besides Ham who had no rider to actually jump bodies should the opportunity arise.

"There won't really be a need for any of that," Major J started. "That's what I've been trying to tell you. The General wants to offer you the use of his Gulfstream II private jet. It can fly 500 miles an hour, carry 12 passengers, and is ready for take-off at Executive Park which is about 15 minutes from here."

"Whoa, we're moving a little too fast for my taste here," Frank called out. "We, at least I, need to think this through before I can allow my young charge and my wife to go tearing off half-way across the country to fight..." And then he just ran down.

"Yes darling, it *is* what we just did; and extremely well, I might add," Clara said lovingly.

"I say let's take it to them," Ham called fervently.

When Frank still looked hesitant, Camael placed a hand on his forearm and spoke softly. "There has been far too much dying for one night and I fear it is not over yet. Frank, you have died twice this evening and I fully understand your hesitation to..."

"No," Frank growled loudly, yanking his arm away. "I don't care a whit about what happens to me, it comes with the shield. What I can't stand again, what I refuse to witness again..." and his voice broke. Tears broke free from his eyes, coursing their way down his dusty, haggard cheeks. "I can't stand to see *you* die again," he pleaded, looking at Clara.

"I almost lost my mind a little while ago and was ready to charge into the gate myself. I wanted to kill anything that stood for the other side because they had taken the only person who has ever meant anything to me." Hanging his head he whispered softly, "I went into a complete berserker rage; I lost all control. I don't want to ever do that again."

Clara moved her chair to her husband's side and took his hand gently. "I felt exactly the same way *both* times you died honey, and I railed against Raquel to let me loose, to let me use her power. It's really a good thing she refused," she said with a sheepish grin.

Frank leaned down and gently kissed his wife's lips, softly at first, and then with increasing ardor. When he finally broke contact, Clara's eyes flashed white and Raquel said, "He really is a dynamite kisser."

The lighthearted jest broke the heavy tension in the air and everyone laughed a little nervously at first. But when Frank threw back his head and let loose a belly laugh, everyone joined in earnestly. Once the laughter had died out Frank turned to Major J and said, "Let's get to the airplane. The night's not over yet."

"A PLEASURE TO MEET you General," Frank said as they mounted the stairs built into the door of the aircraft. "I must say, when Major J told me your airplane was equipped with a wheelchair lift and tiedowns, I was overjoyed."

"Please call me Hiram, otherwise I'll have to call you lieutenant all the time," the General grinned. "My late wife was wheelchair bound for the last eight years, and we spent a lot of time travelling the world and seeing the sights," he sighed. "I did my best to empty her bucket list before she went over to the other side." His eyes took on a distant look and Frank waited politely until he was finished with his memory. Shaking himself Hiram said, "Anyway, you should get both Hamilton and your wife secured while I finish pre-flighting her," he said, turning back to the cockpit.

"You're the pilot?" Frank replied to the unexpected announcement.

"I've logged over two thousand hours in this beauty since I bought her ten years ago and I've been multi-engine qualified for over forty years," he said with a twinkle in his eyes. "Flew C-130's for the better part of them," he added.

The brilliance of his gaze belied the weather-beaten appearance of his face. This man was an old warhorse and he was far from finished. Frank nodded and turned toward the rear of the plane to ensure all was in order. Ham and Clara were both secured to spots where seats had been hastily removed from the equipment rails on the floor. The remaining ten seats were filled with the other members of the team. Four rugged and totally capable-looking men with long beards, short haircuts, and steel in their eyes sat passively waiting.

Daniel surfaced from Hofniel's control for a moment to ask them, "Where did you guys serve?"

The oldest-looking of the four turned to him and said, "Fallujah."

"Al-Zarqawi?" Daniel asked in return referring to Abu Musab al-Zarqawi, the chief strategist and Al-Qaeda leader behind the insurgents in Iraq during the battles for the city of Fallujah.

The man pointed his chin toward the man across the aisle from him and said, "Kettlebell was on the crew that found the bastard so the wingnuts could take him out," he finished, referring to the Air Force bombing of the safe house in which the terrorist leader had been hiding.

"So you guys all served together?" Daniel asked.

"Major J, all of us, Hell, most everyone in our unit now served under the General when he was CO of the Regiment. We're all Palehorse," he concluded.

Daniel's sharp intake of breath belied his calm exterior. He realized he was in the presence of some of the most seasoned counter-terrorist members the Marine Corps had ever seen.

"How about you?" Kettlebell asked. "You look pretty hard yourself."

Daniel hesitated for a moment before pulling a large gold coin from his pocket. He held it up for the others to see the skull impressed onto its surface with the number 6 on the forehead.

"Hoowee, lookee here boys," Crowed Kettlebell. "We got us a *genuine* Navy Frogman in our midst."

When Daniel colored darkly the older man cut Kettlebell a hard look that silenced him immediately.

"Sorry Gunny," was all he said.

"Where?" Gunny asked.

"Gardez, Turkman, Kandahar, Jbad, Kabul; three tours," was all he answered, but it was enough.

Kettlebell leaned forward and held his closed fist out; Daniel bumped his own fist against it. "We cool?" he asked.

"Yeah," Daniel replied. Then Hofniel's eyes flared bronze and both Marines jerked their heads back. "We're cool," he said.

Major J stepped into the front of the airplane cabin from the cockpit and announced, "Strap in, we're wheels up in 10."

TWENTY-NINE

"WE'LL BE ON THE GROUND 30 minutes before dawn," Major J was explaining as they sat facing each other in the forward part of the cabin. "The local unit has three vehicles waiting for us; two vans with lifts and a Hummer for the rest." Looking at Frank he continued.

"With your concurrence we'll put you, Clara, Sharon, and McElroy in one van, and Ham, Marrisa, Jason, and Daniel in the second. My squad and I will follow in the Hummer with the General." For whatever reason the Major couldn't bring himself to address the vessels as their rider's names.

Frank nodded. "Raquel is an Archangel and McElroy is God's Wrath, so we're well protected. Plus Arariel, who does amazing things with weak-willed people."

"I have to tell you, in just the brief time Cassiel was my rider I understood how all this works; but it still creeps me out," he said, shuddering visibly. "It just isn't natural for an angel, especially an Archangel, to occupy a human's body."

"We've been helping humanity fight against the forces of true evil for nearly six thousand years," Camael remarked. "Long before the Shang Dynasty was organized or Upper and Lower Egypt were united. And it's the only way we can manifest in this plane of existence."

"How does that happen anyway?" Gunny asked in earnest. "I mean if one of the *vessels* gets killed how do we keep the angel here to continue the fight?" For him it was pure logistics. Keep as many power pieces on the board as possible at all times.

"Unless it's a moment of dire necessity we try to assimilate into the volunteers mind slowly to avoid the shock you experienced," Raquel explained. "But as we've already discovered tonight we *can* even enter into the body of an effectively dead host if prior permission has been granted," she continued, smiling at Frank to ease the painful memory of that incident.

"So does that mean you can bring someone back to life if they've given you permission before it happens?" Gunny pressed the question, leaning forward in his seat.

"So it would seem, although we are hardly in the practice of doing so under routine circumstances," Camael interjected. "We too, have certain guidelines we're expected to follow; certain tenants to which we must adhere." He smiled. "And it *kind of creeps me out* as well to think of jumping from one host to another to simply repair whatever damage has been done to their flesh."

"Sure, but as a leader you can see why that concept appeals to me?" Gunny pressed.

Nodding, Camael replied, "Yes, as a leader I see the value of the practice."

"Then let's make it official," Gunny pushed the issue. Looking around at his three compatriots he asked, "Any of my guys *not* want an Archangel to jump in and bring you back to life if you bite the big one tonight?" All three Marines gave Gunny an immediate thumbs up. "Then it's official; you have permission from all four of us to jump in if you feel the need."

"Anyway, keeping Ham safe is mission one," Frank continued, steering the conversation back to the division of personnel on the ground once they arrived. "So we need to send him, Azrael who is the Angel of Death, Hofniel who is God's favored Warrior, and Camael the Archangel to protect him. And we need to send them wherever Sariel, Priscilla's angel, and Uriel are. I have a feeling Ham and Pris are the key to finishing this whole disaster."

A tone chimed and Major J stood. "That means were on long final. We'll be on the ground in ten."

"THE GATE IS AT A PLACE called the Cordorus Furnace," Ariel informed them when they landed at Donegal Springs Airpark. "It's a 30 minute drive but only 19 miles. The rural roads around here originated as market cart trails and many aren't much improved," he said with a knowing grin.

He was an older man in his mid-50s with a flowing mane of tawny golden-brown hair and a self-assured posture. He was built like he had worked as a pipe fitter most of his life, with arms the size of small trees.

"Then we should get moving," Frank replied coolly.

Once everyone was situated in the vehicles the caravan moved. Frank yielded his driver position to the local militia member whose group had provided the vans. He obviously knew the roads and alternate routes better than any of the Oklahoma crew. Ariel chose to ride in the back of the van with Raquel and they chatted animatedly. When they had been moving about ten minutes Raquel called to Frank.

"Frank, Ariel is Father's Lion and he is fearless in the face of any odds. He would not tell you so himself as we do not boast of our titles, but he will not desert you in the hardest of times. Father has asked him to be your partner and he has something to share with you."

"I have some local information about the site if you think it will help," he offered.

"Let's hear it," Frank replied.

Now that they were nearing the point of confrontation he had retreated to his warrior mode; he was calm and collected but nearly stone-faced.

"The Cordorus Furnace is an historical landmark. It was built in 1765 by William Bennet to provide foundry work for the area," Ariel quoted as if he'd read a tourist guide. "As such it has thick walls built of local stone, cut by master masons. It sets in front of heavy woods next to an active creek and isn't far from the Susquehanna River."

Frank nodding his understanding of the tactical location. "It once boasted a furnace and it is from there the gate has been opened. Many demons and several wraiths are loose in the countryside and the local militia group hunts them in earnest. The area for 15 miles in every direction is sparsely populated."

"Who guards the gate?" Raquel asked.

"Adriel and Ariel are there with Sariel and Uriel," he answered. "Theirs has been a valiant effort but the gate was already active when we arrived. None others have entered this veil since our arrival but we know not the number before us."

"How many militia in the woods and are they the only humans out there?" Frank asked.

"The militia commander is Colonel Jeremiah Goldsmith, U.S. Army retired, and he has forty seasoned members in his group," Ariel provided. "They are mostly retired military, police officers, and two Federal Agents but they're all still very good at what they are doing. There is also a Game Warden who is involved although I do not fully comprehend her role."

"Do any of the members own or have access to a drone with FLIR capability?" Frank asked as he ran through the standard escapee search protocols he had used many times.

Ariel produced a cell phone from his jacket pocket and punched in a number. Handing the phone to Frank he said, "This is Colonel Goldsmith's number I just called."

"Goldsmith," the voice at the other end answered.

"Colonel, Lieutenant Frank Kratos from Oklahoma. We're the..."

"I'll save you the time Frank," Goldsmith cut him off. "I know as much as I need to about you and this incident thanks to your janitor and...how the hell does a thirteen-year-old manage to get an Archangel rider anyway? Never mind, I like Priscilla, she's a spitfire. How far out are you?"

"Probably 15 minutes but I need to know if anyone has access to a drone with FLIR," Frank asked again.

"Negative," Goldsmith replied. "Wouldn't do any good, canopy is too thick for any thermal imaging. Good idea though. We've got something better; tracking dogs. Three of the unit's members train search and rescue dogs and they're hot on the trail. I'm getting regular reports of confrontations and some of my men are totally spooked. Some of the things they've killed defy the imagination. But they're soldiering on and we'll have them mopped up eventually."

"Speaking of SAR, have you been able to establish a perimeter?" Frank asked next.

"Normally I'd take offense to someone trying to tell me my business but this isn't normal; not by any stretch of the mind," the Colonel chuckled. "We've got four-man teams of local LEOs and a few State Troopers at every goat path and rabbit trail leading away from Hellam Township out to thirty miles. All they know is there may be some dangerous wild animals which have escaped from a circus travelling through the area."

"It took some convincing but they've allowed us to take the lead," he continued. "Our story is; we're the security team the circus hired to find and capture their loose beasts. They're on high alert which is the best we can do. No sense getting them all worked up over something most of them wouldn't believe anyway."

"Copy that sir," Frank replied with growing admiration. This man knew his business.

"Colonel, if you don't mind my asking how is it *you're* not sideways on this whole situation?" Frank asked curiously.

"You mean why am I not scared spitless by what I've seen and heard?" Goldsmith replied. "Same as you only I was on the *Army's* paranormal research team. Twelve years at Area 51 as Security Program Administrator. Alien is alien regardless of where they originate."

"So you were in charge of the *Cammo Dudes*?" Frank fished.

Well-played, Lieutenant; but they were only a small portion of my security forces," Goldsmith retorted.

"Well at least aliens aren't bent on the devastation of the planet and enslavement of the human race," Frank reminded him.

"Not that *you* know of," Goldsmith replied nonchalantly.

"SISTER, IT IS VERY good you have made the journey here," Uriel said as Raquel rolled off of the lift. "I fear we may need every Brother and Sister before the day is done. Can you sense the activity?" he asked, indicating the foundry.

Priscilla came running from somewhere in the woods, leaping and dancing as she made her way across the open grass around the building. "Ham, I'm so glad to see you," she effused as he rolled off the lift from the van he was in. Dropping to her knees she hugged him fiercely and pulled her head back, locking eyes with him for a moment before kissing him soundly on the mouth.

"Priscilla?" The exclamation burst out of Marissa's startled mouth.

"Mom, excellent, you're here as well," Pris said, looking at her mother without rising from her position next to Ham. "Sariel says we're going to need every hand to prevent the coming attack."

"Don't you think you're being just a little forward?" Marrisa asked her daughter. "I mean, here in front of all these strangers?"

"Mom, there are no strangers in these woods tonight except for the demons we hunt," Priscilla replied matter-of-factly. "And we could all be dead before sunset. So I'm not wasting any time," and she leaned over to kiss Ham again.

"Well alrighty then," Ham crowed. "Which way is the fight?"

As he turned his chair toward the foundry building all the angel vessels turned to face him. Each in turn placed their closed right fist across their chest, centered over their hearts, and bowed their heads slightly.

"What?" Ham asked, bewildered.

"All my Brothers, Sisters, and Cousins can sense the immense power you wield Hamilton and they pledge you fealty," Sariel spoke. "We need to prepare you for the coming battle; to engage our power with yours so as to have the best chance to prevail."

"Hey, I just sent Amom to the Moon and he was one big, bad dude," Ham smiled. "I figure whatever they throw at us, together we can handle. We got this," he said with confidence.

"Amom was indeed a formidable opponent," Uriel said, walking up with Raquel beside him in Clara's wheelchair. "But we all sense the same forces at work on the other side of this open portal. Leviathan amasses his horde and Abaddon the Destroyer comes. Five other Archdemons are joined in. Mammon who searches out greed in every heart, Amayon the King of East Hell, Corson the King of West Hell, Ziminiar the King of North Hell, and Astaroth, the *Grand Duke of All Legions of the Pit*. Their numbers are truly legion and if we fail in closing the gate before they arrive, all is lost."

THIRTY

"THIS LOOKS JUST LIKE the gate in Texas," Ham said upon entering the forge. "I closed that easily enough. Why would this one be any different?"

Uriel had cautioned him against displaying any power until they were all ready and positioned to engage the gate as one. "The gate was held open in Texas by Amom and his horde," he explained. "Once he was vanquished the gate had very little energy to sustain itself."

"So this gate is being held open by the combined power of all the Archdemons you just mentioned?" Ham asked softly, almost in a whisper.

"They can't hear you Ham," Azrael said kindly. "And currently only Abaddon holds the portal in place. Once opened it takes much less energy to maintain. This is why we must assert all our power simultaneously to close it," she continued solemnly. "We may very well get only one chance to do so."

Ham found himself dead center in front of the blazing gate with angels and Archangels ranked to either side. Sariel had positioned the various vessels in points fanned across the front of the furnace based on their abilities and levels of power.

"Let us prepare," he ordered.

Frank had taken up a guarding position at the entrance to the foundry with Ariel at his side. Frank held his AR rifle at low ready and Ariel clutched a wicked-looking battle-ax in both meaty hands.

"That's an up-close-and-personal weapon," Frank observed. "Wouldn't it be better to end them before they get this close?"

"Yours is the weapon for *ending them*," Ariel replied. "I am here should any get close enough to physically threaten you."

"So I'm in this firefight alone?" Frank blurted incredulously.

"I wouldn't say alone," came a reply from over his shoulder.

Turning, Frank was met with a welcome sight. Four fully-armed, camouflage-wearing soldiers and an aging man with ramrod-straight posture and military written all over him approached from around the building.

"Colonel Goldsmith?" Frank presumed.

"My pleasure Frank," the Colonel replied. "Positions boys," he added, and each man took up a defensive place around the entrance to the foundry. "I've got four more on the other side even though there's no entrance," he informed Frank. "Here, you might need this," he added, holding out a ballistic vest.

Frank visibly relaxed, donning the vest before leaning back against the door frame of the entrance. "Now I guess we just wait until they either close it or not," he said, gesturing behind him with his head.

"And if they don't we'll be doing a rear-facing action posthaste," the Colonel replied.

"Amen," Frank agreed.

"GENERAL, I DON'T MEAN any disrespect sir but you shouldn't be out here," Major J said.

"Evan, I've lived a full life and seen or done more than any ten men I know. This is the final conflict between good and evil, at least in my lifetime," the General replied grinning. "I wouldn't miss this for anything."

"Gunny, send two men around that thicket. I saw something moving in there," Major J said. The six of them worked as a light squad and had done so many times before.

Gunny motioned to Kettlebell and another man who flanked the heavily grown underbrush and disappeared around both sides. Moments later three quick shots were fire and the foliage burst open to allow passage for a gorilla-sized creature with hairless red skin and tiger paws. It stopped for an instant, saw the four men, and charged. Weapons erupted from the four and the creature was haloed in a momentary spray of green fluid and gobbets of flesh before it crashed to the ground. The General walked closer and put a well-aimed pistol round into the top of its head.

Hofniel, Arariel, and Hemah stepped carefully over a fallen tree as they made their way down a game trail between the Codorus Furnace and the Susquehanna River. None of them spoke but each was apprehensive about the next demon they might encounter. They had slain seven thus far and knew not how many more were around them. They also knew there were human hunting teams in the woods as well, some with tracking dogs.

They were certain this all made the demons which had come through the gate very agitated, in turn making them even more aggressive. All in all it made for very anxious work. Each carried a pistol in a holster but Hofniel still carried the street sweeper, Hemah had his riot gun, and Arariel held her crossbow. It had actually been more effective against two of the seven than had been the shotguns. They were a good team.

Screaming like a jungle cat a black figure dropped onto Hemah's back and sunk impossibly long fangs into the back of his neck, tearing out his spine in one motion. Hofniel opened up with the shotgun, blasting three one ounce lead slugs into its torso but the cat-thing only crouched to pounce at him. A bolt from Arariel's weapon struck through its ear and out the bottom of its jaw. Writhing in a blur of fury the demon thrashed about in front of them for 30 seconds before succumbing to its wounds.

Turning to Hemah's ravaged neck, they watched as it regenerated. Nerves reformed, blood vessels grew back, and the spinal column stacked one vertebra onto another. Finally muscle tissue and skin covered the cervical spine and McElroy gasped a coughing breath.

"Mother of God that hurt," Patrick exclaimed. Then his eyes brightened and Hemah was back in charge. The three moved off into the woods.

Cassiel's vessel was a young black male, vibrant and full of energy. He fully emulated the definition of his name; God's Anger and Speed. Adriel's vessel was a quiet middle-aged woman with dark hair and features. As one of the fourteen Angels of Death, she also appeared her part. Between the two, they were desolation on the move.

In the woods walking along Cordorus Creek they saw a ghostly figure misting through the trees. The figure oriented toward them and sped in their direction. Both angels knew this to be a wraith and what to do to thwart it. Joining hands they began the incantation which Raquel had told them worked against her wraith.

As the figure approached they extended their hands toward the spirit form and shouted the culminating phrase. The figure bounced away into the dawning sky as if it had struck a wall before zooming straight back down at them. Unprepared for this result, they began the incantation again but with inadequate time. The wraith flew straight into Adriel's vessel and the young woman dropped to the ground in convulsions.

As Cassiel reached for her a voice called, "I wouldn't do that."

Turning toward the sound he spied a young woman in a green and brown uniform approaching on the run. She tossed him a canister as she approached and said, "Shake this all over her body."

The woman was busy pulling a strip of cloth and a length of fibrous twine from her backpack. She tied the cloth around the thrashing woman's head before lashing Adriel's feet and hands together with the opposite ends of the twine. Then she stepped back and shouted, "*Discedite, spiritus malum.*"

The wraith figure exploded from Adriel's chest and flew in circles around them screaming like a banshee. The uniformed woman pointed both hands at the wraith and shouted the same command again. This time the wraith went silent and spun in a vicious circle, faster and faster, until it became a blurred ball. Then it popped out of sight.

"Really, all you have to do is shout *depart evil spirit* and they go away?" Cassiel asked, looking askance at the woman.

"That and tie a piece of a burial shroud around their head and bind their hands and feet with pure hemp fiber blessed by a holy man," she answered, grinning. "And douse them liberally with kosher salt."

"And you just happen to be carrying these items around with you?" Cassiel shot back.

"Yes, because I just happened to be in the woods hunting supernatural creatures and had those items with me," she retorted in kind.

"Well thank you, that was very kind of you to come to my aid," Adriel said from the ground. "Now, seeing as how my partner would rather suspiciously *question* our savior rather than thank her *or* help me, would you mind untying me and telling me your name?"

My name is Kristine Tomlinson and I'm the local Game Warden," she answered as she removed the binding fibers. "I'm also the resident *ghost buster.*"

I am Cassiel, Father's Anger," he replied, "My cousin on the ground is Adriel, Father's Help to Mankind. Your people also refer to her as the Angel of Death."

"She certainly looks the part," Kristine replied, pursing her lips. "Do you two have people names?"

"My vessel is called Marston Goodman and Adriel's is Angela Peabody. We prefer Cassiel and Adriel if you don't mind. When you call their names it alerts our vessel owners," Cassiel explained. "They experience everything we do but remain disconnected. When they hear their name they naturally attempt to respond which confuses the vessel for a moment. Right now we can't spare any such moments."

"Fine, Cassiel and Adriel it is," Kristine replied. "You two want some company?"

"WHEN I GIVE THE WORD we must all focus our combined energies on the portal," Sariel said, standing next to Ham with her hand on his shoulder.

"Why aren't we all holding hands or touching like we did at the hospital?" Ham asked her.

"Our combined power is most likely too much for your mind to channel," she replied. "It is also safer this way. Also, if anything happens to any one of us the combined total will be less impacted."

"What could happen?" Ham asked with consternation clear in his voice.

"Anything could happen, Ham," Uriel spoke up. "The longer we wait the greater chance the forces of the Pit will start their march. We really *must do this now*."

"Just so," Sariel said. "Together now," he began, turning toward the pulsating reddish-orange ball hanging three feet off the floor of the foundry.

A figure emerged from the portal; then another. Suddenly a veritable flood of misshapen creatures and twisted forms began pouring forth.

"NOW!" Sariel yelled.

Varying shades of purple, magenta, white, gold, and bronze coalesced into a shimmering rainbow of power and energy. The column of light impacted the portal soundlessly but the power released upon contact rocked everyone in the room and caused the building to tremble on its foundation.

Ham felt his chair tip dangerously but Sariel had never moved her hand from his shoulder and Uriel was standing on the other side. Azrael stood behind him next to her daughter with one hand on a handle on his chair while Camael stood beside her holding the other handle.

"Yeah," Ham exclaimed excitedly. The figures which had already emerged were instantly pulverized into dust by the overwhelming might of the combined celestial power and the portal flickered, wavering.

"Do not relent," Sariel called to everyone. "Remain focused; concentrate."

Clara's wheelchair was next to Uriel and he held his Sister's hand. Fierce white light surrounded the five angelic beings and the Prophet. Power was tangible, audible and visible in the awesome display of righteous might.

Ham extended his hand, struggling to close it into a fist as if he were trying to close his grip on some unseen force. Beads of sweat broke out onto his face and his breath came in ragged gasps. And yet he refused to relent. His face reddening with the effort, his hand slowly, inexorably closed. A sound like the shorting of a high voltage circuit ripped the still dawn and the flash of power accompanying it bedazzled every eye.

When their vision cleared the only light in the room was the pale gray of approaching sunrise. But even by that light, everyone could see the five bizarre figures standing where the portal had been. "Hello, Brothers and Sisters," one of them said.

THIRTY-ONE

"ABADDON, THIS IS NOT your world," Sariel said softly but firmly. "We cannot allow you to wreak havoc on those Father has foresworn us to protect."

"I have no intention of asking your permission Brother, so you won't need to *allow* it," Abaddon hissed as he thrust his clasped hands at Uriel.

The change of focus caught almost everyone off guard; everyone except Ham. His hand was up and deflected the force of Abaddon's power even as it crossed the brief space. All five of the Archdemons pulled up short. Each had started a step forward as if theirs had been a preconceived assault. Ziminiar, first to recover from the unexpected intervention of a frail, human invalid, cast a bolt of power unconcealed directly at Ham. Camael deflected it over Ham's right shoulder even as Ham was bringing his own force to bear.

Then all five Archdemons unleashed their power at Archangels across the room indiscriminately. Flashes and pulses of force and energy flew around the room knocking stones loose from the walls and rattling the heavy wooden timbers of the roof.

Camael was the first to be struck down and Uriel immediately stepped over his still form while he recovered the damage done to his host. Pressing the issue Abaddon threw burst upon burst of energy at Camael's still form which Uriel deflected until the last one. Camael had just drawn a breath and sat upright when the force of power behind Abbadon's assault broke through Uriel's defense. Camael was thrown seated into the wall behind them. The sickening thud told all of his demise. The body of Jason Omikawa had been crushed beyond recovery.

Uriel unleashed a volley of energy bolts at Abaddon who, having been weakened by his onslaught, was attempting to hide inside one of the furnace alcoves. Uriel stopped him with a blow from his side and continued to punish him with bolts of force rained down upon his bowed back until he screamed once and succumbed. Abaddon's figure dissolved into nothingness.

Meanwhile Sariel and Raquel had each engaged Mammon and Amayon on one end of the large room. Their nearly equal power had created a roiling wall of pulsing and crackling light which lit the interior of the room like strobes. Seeking to separate the two Archangels, Mammon stepped away from Amayon while continuing his assault.

But Sariel instead leapt across the space behind the two wheelchairs, positioning himself on Raquel's immediate right. The combination of their similar white sparkling energy flows combined into one and instantly pulverized Mammon. Amayon, with an extreme effort of will, poured all his energy into defending himself against this overpowering force while trying to move back toward the portal. But the portal was no longer open and the Archdemons of the Pit realized they were now stranded in a different world.

Recognizing the hopelessness of his situation Amayon bellowed his rage as he forged his way across the room, one surging step at a time. Against the bombardment he was suffering his very essence began to waver and then to shred. Strips of flesh began to peel off his face and chest and fear took up residence on his features.

Screaming his rage once more he tried even harder to resist; and exploded. Fragments of his form were thrown around the room like confetti at a hero's welcome. His intact head ricocheted off a roof timber and struck the concrete floor with a resounding splat. Lifeless eye seemed to still glare at them with unveiled malevolence.

At the same time the others were engaged Ham and Azrael were wrestling with Corson. Unfamiliar with their techniques, Ham was trying to use brute force to overcome him. Corson simply continued to deflect the blunt force efforts Ham threw at him and Ham was tiring. Sensing this, Corson moved in for the kill only to find a lesser angel barring his way.

"Aside pest," Corson commanded, flipping his hand and tossing Azrael onto the ground.

When Ham saw Marrisa as Azrael's vessel cast aside his anger boiled over. Face reddening and eyes bulging, Ham cast bolts of force at Corson in an unendurable barrage of raw, uncontrolled power. Even as Corson continued to deflect every assault he was forced across the room toward the doorway. Ariel stepped through the opening behind him and buried his battle-ax in the back of Corson's skull. Frank had sent Ariel to help, as the few glimpses of the conflict he saw did not appear to be going well for the good guys.

Ziminiar stepped next to his fallen compatriot and blasted Ariel. Flinging his battle-ax up in front of his face, Ariel deflected the energy blast but knew he would not survive another. Raising the weapon over his head, he stepped into the blow as Ziminiar unleashed another bolt of force.

His aim was spoiled even at that close range by a surge of power cast against him by Azrael. She stepped up next to Ariel, shoulder to shoulder, and they linked hands in defense against Ziminiar's volley. Their forms began to waver and Azrael's hair burst into flames and singed off. Screaming, she continued to press against the storm of power being showered upon them. Ariel's clothing began to smolder and they knew they were soon dead.

Then a form struck Ziminiar and both figures burst into flames before them. Aghast, they stood staring until Ariel realized his shirt had ignited and he began beating at it. Both looked at the pile of smoldering flesh and realized the form of Carl the janitor was one of them. Azrael rubbed her hands over her scorched scalp and felt the hair already beginning to grow back as the peeling scalp flaked off in her hands.

"He sacrificed himself to save us," she shuddered. "Why?"

"Because that was the charge from our Father," Raquel said, looking sadly at Carl's lifeless body while tears streamed down her face. "I should not be sad; I will see my Brother again once I return home." A blast of energy glanced off the wall beside them and all three heads turned to see Astaroth forming another ball of energy to cast.

"I shall destroy you all and then I will devour this Prophet," he growled.

Raising his hands he threw the second energy pulse at Raquel, Azrael, and Ariel after Ham had blocked the first. Ariel leapt forward with his battle-ax and met the energy head-on, with devastating results. The mild-mannered, well-muscled man of 50 was pulverized by the force. He had stopped the blast but paid for the respite with his life.

Ham's answering bolt of rage and fury knocked Astaroth against the wall of the furnace but he only recoiled from the wall and cast his own pulse of energy. Ham flicked it aside almost casually and went to work on the final Archdemon. Astaroth matched him bolt for bolt and tormented him while they exchanged power.

"How is it Father has chosen one so weak to be his Prophet?" the vile demon taunted. "Could he not have at least chosen a *whole* human being?" the hideous creature continued. "This one can only wield power with *one hand*," he jeered.

Ham was not affected by the taunts. "I've spent most of my life listening to bullies like you talk about how inadequate I am," he said, forcing Astaroth back against the wall yet again.

Astaroth recovered but less quickly this time. "Is that the best you have, crippled mortal?" he sneered. "Soon I shall tire of this game and I will erase you from existence," he challenged, responding with a salvo of force.

Ham cast every volley and thrust aside while continuing to blast his own torrent of power at the Archdemon. "You should have studied your victims a little more thoroughly," he called. "Then you would have known we humans are at our best when our backs are against the wall."

As he poured a fusillade of energy into the Grand Duke of Hell he remembered the kindness Uriel had shown him at the hospital. He saw Camael's face as he recognized Ham as God's Prophet and announced it as such. And he saw Sariel, standing now and watching the battle with awe. His future stood there in the form of his love, Priscilla. Yes, he realized he was in fact deeply in love with that sassy, spirited young woman.

This acknowledgement strengthened his resolve and he pulled out all the stops.

"I don't know about everybody else but I'm tired of your mouth," Ham said. "Put up or shut up."

He unleashed the full spectrum of light, power, and energy God had given him to wield with his servant's heart. A coruscating deluge of brilliant silver light engulfed the struggling form of the Archdemon for a moment and then the room went dark.

As the dazzle from the fireworks wore off and they began to see again in the dim light, Raquel turned her chair to the others and said, "It is finished."

THIRTY-TWO

"THE HIGHWAY PATROL reports they fired on a *bear* which attacked one of their checkpoints from out of the woods but they were unable to find it after it ran back in," Cassiel told the gathered assembly. "I'm guessing they didn't really look that hard because some of the troopers said it was the wrong color for a bear and others said it didn't sound or move like a bear."

They had lost God's Lion Ariel and the Archangels Camael and Uriel, leaving them with three fatalities of human form to deal with. One could have been explained away to the local authorities but three were going to be problematic. Fortunately only one was a local resident, so that made it easier to only report one fatality. The fact he was in his 50s and out on an *escaped animal hunt* lent credence to the story of his falling off a ledge to his death. Jason and Carl's bodies would be buried in a nearby cemetery long-forgotten by history in unmarked graves.

"As much as I don't like it, telling the department Jason decided to move on after the injuries he suffered in the assault on my house will have to do," Frank said sullenly. "He deserves a hero's funeral with full police honors."

"I agree, but the autopsy required by state and local statute would produce results that he was crushed, and that would open an investigation," the General replied. "Add to it his body would be completely through rigor and livor mortis would show we moved it. Too many questions we can't answer," he concluded.

"With that said I'd like to offer a memorial service at our compound for those in the know who would like to attend," the General continued after a moment's thought. "We'll set it up for a week or so from now; give you a chance to get settled back in Oklahoma. He'll have full honors of our own making but it'll be something to see, I promise you."

"What about Carl?" Sariel asked.

"Because Uriel used both of us as vessels, whenever I got near Carl it was almost like I could read his mind or at least be more familiar with him," Azrael offered. "As far as I can tell he had no family and no close friends. He didn't socialize much and had only worked at the hospital for a couple of years."

She smiled softly before adding, "Being on the night shift by request made him almost invisible. The only reason Dr. Pashteen knew him was because the good doctor preferred the late shift as well. I'm sure some of the nursing staff might recognize him but I doubt if any will miss him. That's kind of sad, you know?" Azrael finished, shaking her head.

Hofniel walked in from the woods followed by Hemah and Arariel, who were walking very close together. He stopped at the perimeter of the group as if silently seeking permission to speak. The other two continued on into the privacy of the foundry.

"How are we looking out there?" Frank asked Hofniel.

"There have been a few more sightings but I believe we have tracked down and eliminated the majority of them," he replied.

"What happens to the ones we don't track down," Frank wanted to know.

"They are not of this realm," Raquel replied for Hofniel. "Without a host vessel they will perish within a matter of hours."

"So even if we don't find them, as long as they don't find a vessel, they die?" Frank clarified.

"Indeed," Sariel interjected. "Without a vessel from this plane, none of us can survive more than a handful of hours."

"When will we return to the airport?" Hofniel asked quietly.

For once Frank didn't have an answer. "There are too many variables yet for me to answer that," he hedged. "I'll need to confer with the Colonel and you General, to get a better idea." They walked off to find Colonel Goldsmith.

THE COLONEL WAS CONFERRING with his two platoon leaders when they found him.

"I have one dead and two wounded, one seriously," one of the subordinates was saying as they approached.

Goldsmith nodded and looked to the other leader who said, "I have two missing, presumed dead. They're not responding to radio contact and their beacons are inactive."

"Continue the search," the Colonel replied. Looking to the first leader, he added, "Send every available man to the search area and establish a grid search pattern. I want a definite status of some sort by nightfall. I'll contact the local authorities and report the man killed by the *wild animal attack*."

"Yes sir," they both responded, standing at attention and whipping a salute.

After their leader snapped to attention and returned the motion, the two moved off at a jog. Turning to the General, Goldsmith offered a salute of his own in respect of his superior rank. General Martin braced to attention and returned it crisply.

"Unless you need us for anything further from my squad we need to RTB, Jeremiah," Hiram informed him.

"General, I believe we've got this," he replied. "I appreciate you bringing the key players in and the support of your *specialists*," he finished with a wry grin.

"They were just doing what they've been trained to do," the General replied. "And to tell the God's honest truth, I haven't seen them this excited and happy since Desert Storm II."

During the search for the remaining demons the four-man Marine Whitehorse Recon team had successfully tracked and eliminated no less than two dozen creatures from Hell.

"My guys were pretty jazzed to have just been able to follow them around," Jeremiah replied. "Seems as though they've picked up a few new skills."

"Then we'll be leaving," Hiram said. He extended his hand to Jeremiah and grinned. "Good hunting," he said.

ANGEL VESSELS SURROUNDED Ham and the two remaining Archangels when Frank and Hiram returned to the foundry. As they approached, Hemah and Arariel were coming out of the building and they were holding hands.

"I wonder what that's all about," Frank remarked to Hiram.

Having overheard them, Raquel replied as if the question had been directed at her. "As we are strictly energy beings we do not experience the wide array of physical stimulation humans do," she said. "When given the opportunity, and only with the willing concurrence of the host vessels, we like to experience as many of these physical sensations as possible."

Frank looked startled; in fact he and Hiram were both taken aback.

Sariel laughed outright. "If you two could see you're faces," she chortled.

"I...that is to say...didn't realize you could," Frank stammered.

"Be intimate?" Raquel finished politely. "Do you think I just close my eyes and cover my ears when you and Clara make love?"

"Oh that's just wrong," Frank exclaimed, reddening at the sudden realization.

"Why do you think I said we both love you," Raquel responded, clearly enjoying his discomfort.

"Well, I thought it was because I'm a generally nice guy, you know, and love Clara with all my heart," he replied.

"Well, that too," she replied giggling.

Blushing even brighter, Frank turned and walked quickly out of sight around the foundry.

"I think you enjoy embarrassing him Sister," Sariel commented.

"Perhaps just a little Sister," Raquel replied.

Apparently both the Archangels were letting their hair down a little now that the threat of a demonic conflagration had passed. Until this point Ham had said very little since the defeat of Astaroth. He now cleared his throat and turned his chair to face Sariel squarely.

"I need to speak with Pris," he said quietly.

The light dimmed in her eyes and Priscilla looked at Ham quizzically. "What's up?" she asked. "You do know I can experience everything that happens while Sariel is in control, right?"

"Yes, but Sariel left herself out of the loop intentionally for the discussion we've just had," he replied.

Pris' face grew solemn, then hardened slightly. "When Sariel leaves, will I go back to my crippled form?"

"No, it's nothing like that," Raquel interjected.

"So you're part of this too?" Pris asked, rounding on her teacher.

"We all are," Azrael replied. "It had to be a joint decision and we all agreed," she finished.

"Agreed to what?" Pris asked, now a little frightened.

"There was a human being once who lived as a prophet named Elijah," Ham explained. "He was so important to God that when he died, God made him an angel and named him Metatron. He had a twin brother who was also elevated named Sandalphon. They're the only two humans ever selected for elevation to that level of communion with God and both eventually became Archangels." He paused to ensure she was following.

"So what has that got to do with any of us?" Pris asked curiously.

"Father has asked Ham to become a watcher," Raquel said and then hurried on. "It is the first step toward becoming one of our cousins."

"But how can you be a watcher and still be in...you won't still *be* in human form, will you?" Pris asked; tears and sudden realization springing simultaneously onto her face.

"It doesn't mean I won't be with you anymore," Ham replied. "I'll just be around ... differently," he finished lamely.

Throwing her hands up over her face, Pris turned and ran out of sight around the building.

"Oh that went well," Ham said dejectedly.

THIRTY-THREE

"I'D BE GLAD FOR THE company," Kristine told Marston and Angela. "And most of the training is OJT, you know. I'm sure I'll be busy around her for a while with stragglers."

The pair, as their human personas, had asked their riders for control to approach Kristine as to whether she needed any more hunters and would be willing to train them.

"In fact, let me see if I can find two of my junior hunters and introduce you right now," she continued as she turned and walked away, beckoning them over her shoulder.

Two of Colonel Goldsmith's troops who had been wounded were resting in the rear of an SUV in which the rear seat had been folded down to create a makeshift ambulance. Hammocks had been tied at one end to the shoulder strap mounts for the seatbelts to provide a reclining position for them.

Marston and Angela, meet Michael and Joshua," she said, indicating first one then the other citizen-soldiers.

How's it going?" Michael asked.

"A lot better for me than you apparently," Angela grinned.

Joshua barked out a short laugh before grabbing his side, wincing. "It's okay, it only hurts when I laugh," he said, then laughed again.

Michael gently punched him in the shoulder and said, "Stop, I'll open my field stitches again."

"What happened to you two?" Marston asked.

"Zigged when we should have zagged," Michael replied pan-faced. Then he laughed again, holding his bandaged shoulder.

"We tangled with a demon the size of a moose," Joshua said.

"It was more the size of an elephant," Michael corrected.

"Well it looked more like a moose, even if it was the biggest damn moose I've ever seen," Joshua allowed.

"Did you end it?" Angela asked with what looked like a gleam in her eye.

"It was touch and go for a minute but yeah, we *ended* it alright," Joshua said straight-faced. Then he laughed out loud again, holding his wounded side. Michael was chortling, trying hard not to laugh along with his friend.

Turning to Kristine, Marston asked, "Are these guys on pain meds? Because they're way too happy for a couple of guys who tangled with a super moose demon."

"Ahhhh," Joshua hissed, laughing even harder despite the pain. "Super moose demon, I've got to write that down."

"What is so stinking funny about this whole episode?" Angela inquired. "I can imagine being happy to be alive but you guys are ecstatic."

"Girlie, if you'd just killed, and I do mean *killed*, a super moose demon - I love that name - you'ld be ecstatic just to have survived the situation," Michael crowed. "Oh, the stories we shall tell and the beers which shall be bought in our honor," he exclaimed.

"How did you kill it?" Marston inquired.

Both injured men burst into mirthful chuckles again, causing Angela and Marston to look at Kristine. "If this is what your junior hunters act like I may have to rescind my request," Marston said seriously.

"Guys, out with it or I'll tell them myself," Kristine ordered playfully.

"This monster came thrashing out of the underbrush right on top of us," Joshua began.

"Hooked Josh under the arm and flung him over its shoulder," Michael added. "Must have gone ten feet in the air."

"He opened up on it with his puny 556 and the beastie turned and whacked Mikey right in the shoulder," Joshua continued. "Knocked him tail-over-teakettle down the game trail we were on."

"Josh had only one shot, and it was from *behind*," Michael continued, emphasizing the last word. "And he's got 300 Blackout in his AR. Popped the demon in the backside five times before it could fart." Again the two dissolve into laughter.

"The beast dropped to its knees but immediately tried to get up," Michael said. "So I cross-draw my machete with my good arm and go for the throat."

"I came out of the woods bent over double and Mike was slashing away at this gargantuan's neck like he was cutting firewood," Joshua finished.

"So why is all that so hilarious?" Angela insisted.

"Because two of Josh's bullets went straight up the demon's butt-hole," Michael cried.

And both men spiraled back into gasping fits of laughter again. "We really did *end* it," Michael almost screamed.

"Juveniles," Marston muttered under his breath.

"I like them," Angela countered.

PRIS WAS CRESTFALLEN at the idea of Ham effectively being dead. She couldn't reconcile herself to his becoming a Watcher and decided she had to have it out with him. As she turned to go find him Kristine was standing next to her. Startled, Pris stepped back.

"I saw you standing over here alone and came over to offer my condolences," Kristine said. "I thought at first you had lost someone to a demon. But then I realized you're one of the angel vessels. I remember seeing you all come in early this morning."

"Yes, I'm Sariel's vessel but right now I'm just Priscilla Benton," she said, offering her hand.

"Kristine Tomlinson, local Game Warden and Ghost Buster extraordinaire," she replied, taking Pris' hand and holding it warmly. "Are you okay?"

"No I'm not, not even close," Pris replied. "I've just learned my boyfriend, whom I love desperately, is going to become a Watcher. Which means for all practical purposes he's going to die today."

"How's that again?" Kristine asked, befuddled. Once Pris had explained what she thought she knew, Kristine stood thinking for a moment.

"So you're going back to Oklahoma alone?"

"No, I live with my mom," Pris replied. "Although that's going to be interesting because before I accepted Sariel into my body I was a quadriplegic. That's going to be difficult to explain."

"So don't," Kristine countered.

"Huh?" Pris replied. "What do you mean don't?"

"Just what I said," she replied. "Stay here and become a hunter with me. Looks like I'm starting a local hunter's chapter anyway, seeing as how before today it was me and three others. Now I've got two more and six qualifies for chapter designation."

Now it was Pris' turn to be bewildered. "What are you talking about?"

Once Kristine had explained it all it made perfect sense. Starting a new life in Hellam Township under Kristine's tutelage, using the fighting and perception skills she already had, all eliminated her need to explain her miraculous change to anyone.

And so it was agreed.

THIRTY-FOUR

SHE FOUND HAM SITTING in his chair alone near the entrance to the foundry.

"Where is everyone?" Pris asked casually, walking up behind him.

Startled, Ham relaxed and replied, "They're all doing whatever it takes to get ready for you and your mom to go back to Chickasha with Frank and Clara. The General has offered to drop y'all off at Chickasha Municipal before returning to Lubbock."

"Ham, I love you. You know that, right?" Pris said jumping straight in.

"Sure, and I love you," he replied readily.

"Then how can you leave me like this?" she wailed. "Is it because I'm not in a wheelchair anymore? Because if that's it, I'll ask Sariel..."

"Whoa, whoa, whoa," Ham exclaimed, cutting her off. "You'll do no such thing," he shouted. Seeing her swell up to counter his statement he hurried on. "It has nothing to do with that and it makes my souls sing just knowing you'd even consider giving up your freedom to keep me here. But let me explain everything first before you go ballistic on me, please?" he begged.

At her silent nod, he continued. "I've been offered not only release from this limited form, but immortality," he breathed the last word like a sigh. "No more changing catheter tubes daily; no more bags at all. No more minding what I eat or how much. No more physical therapy every six weeks just to keep my legs and back from becoming infected. You had to do all that and more and now you're free. Can't you see I want to be free too?" He looked at her for a long moment before adding playfully,

"But the best part is this," and entered her mind.

WHEN FRANK WALKED UP on Ham and Priscilla they were staring at each other unspeaking. When he got closer he could see they were both breathing, but he sensed something else was happening. Clara was already loaded on the G II and he had come to tell Priscilla it was time to go. Unsure what to do, he reached for Pris just as she shuddered and staggered backward. Frank grabbed her to steady her.

"Can we do that anytime?" Pris screamed at Ham.

"Uh, huh, any time we want," he replied.

"Can I just kill you now?" she asked playfully.

Frank shouted, "What?" Pris realized he was holding her and his grip had tightened painfully.

"No, no, you don't understand," Pris started.

Then Ham spoke up. "Frank, it's okay, let her go. We just did a Vulcan Mind Meld and she's not herself."

"Boy I'll say. I'm me, and you, and us, and...wow," she breathed.

"Somebody want to tell me what's going on here?" Frank asked brusquely.

"Ham can enter my mind," Pris said simply. "And when he does we can do..." she blushed prettily before continuing. "We can do whatever we want together."

"Ah... ha," Frank said softly, obviously confused.

"Frank, I'm going to become a Watcher but I'm also going to be allowed to maintain a spiritual contact with Pris for the rest of her life until she joins me," Ham explained slowly.

"And that won't be for a long time because God has big plans for me," Pris finished.

"Um, okay," Frank responded. "Is this something we can discuss on the plane? We really do need to be going."

"Oh, I'm not going back with you," Pris replied nonchalantly.

"Your what?...not...but where...your mom...huh?" Frank babbled.

"Exactly," Ham said grinning. "Pris is staying here in Hellam Township. The local hunter leader Kristine has agreed to take on Angela and Marston, the two local vessels for Cassiel and Adriel. When Kristine found Pris crying around back they had a long talk. Pris is going to become a hunter. She still has her ability to see people's colors and their souls. That will be a great skill set for tracking down demons and other nasties."

"Yeah, because apparently Hellam Township is full of things that go bump in the night," Priscilla added.

NOW IT WAS MARRISA'S turn to ask for control of the vessel which Azrael readily relinquished. "Young lady you are not staying here by yourself," she told Pris adamantly.

"I won't be by myself," Pris responded easily. "I'll have Kristine and Marston and Angela and even Beavis and Butthead in the truck."

"I would have to get a power of attorney or legal guardianship or something done up for Kristine, if she's willing, and we need to leave now," Marrisa retorted. "We can discuss this more once we're home."

"Mom, I'm not going back," Pris spoke softly, but there was steel in her voice. "I'm so much more mature than any 13-year-old I would ever meet, and how do we explain my sudden miraculous recovery? I'd be stark-raving buggers inside a week in high school and I'd have to start in a different one anyway. I can home school on the internet; I did most of the time these past two years anyway."

"Priscilla Marie Benson, I am not leaving here without you," Marrisa said harshly.

"Then stay here," Pris replied coolly.

"I just said I'm not...do what?" Marrisa stammered.

"Stay here," she repeated. "You can get a job in Harrisburg just as easily as you did in Chickasha and you could probably help with some of the non-fighting things hunters need."

"And what makes you think I couldn't be a hunter?" Marrisa asked, piqued.

"I...I ...um...didn't say you couldn't," Pris stammered, caught off-guard. "I just didn't think you would want to be."

"Well for your information, Azrael has taught me a lot about being the Angel of Justice and retribution," Marrisa informed them. "I believe I can hold my own against most any demon, given the right training and equipment."

"That hog-leg you still have in your purse would be a good start," Frank said lightly.

"So does that mean you're staying too?" Kristine asked.

"Is there room for one more?" Marrisa asked rhetorically.

"Okay, we're wheels up in 30 minutes," the General shouted. "Load up if you're going," and he turned and stepped into the Hummer.

"What about you Ham?" Pris asked, tears welling in her eyes again. "We can't just leave you sitting here."

Ham turned his chair toward the waiting van and drove onto the lift. "I've got a lot of explaining to do to my dad when I get home," he said. "He'll find someone who can use my chair."

"Your dad," Priscilla gasped. "What are they going to tell him?"

"Nothing, I'm going to tell him myself," Ham responded.

"But you said you weren't going back," Pris started.

"No, I never said that," Ham stopped her. "I said I'm going to become a Watcher. I'm returning to Chickasha so I can see my dad and help him understand everything that's happened in the past month. Once that's all settled he'll simply tell the coroner's office I died in my sleep. It happens all the time," he finished kindly.

Both were silent for long time until Ham said, "How about a kiss goodbye?"

THIRTY-FIVE

"AS SOON AS WE LAND I'm going to go buy a van," Frank said onboard during the flight. "Then we're going house-hunting."

Raquel had left her host as soon as the aircraft door had closed. Clara was looking at him strangely and he returned her level gaze for a moment.

"What, darling?" Frank asked.

"I can't believe Raquel would just leave like that without a goodbye or anything," she said dejectedly.

"Well, she's popped out many times before," Frank countered. "Why is this time any different?"

"Frank, all the other angels are leaving their hosts," Clara explained. "Why would she remain after their mission here on Earth is complete?"

"So you're concerned you may not have her powers anymore?" Frank said, realization dawning on his face.

Clara nodded mutely, a single tear finding its way down her cheek. "I've really enjoyed helping you find lost children and solving cases," she said almost too softly for him to hear.

"Darling, that won't diminish my love for you in the least," he assured her. "And there will be other opportunities for us to work together I'm sure." But he wasn't sure, not really. And so they travelled in silence, each lost in their own thoughts.

Ham had been asleep since shortly after take-off. The ordeal at the Cordorus Furnace had apparently exhausted him, physically and mentally. The return to Chickasha was a solemn one and the General came back into the cabin about 45 minutes into the flight.

"When we touch down at Chickasha, brace for a fast stop," He said. "They've only got five thousand feet of runway."

"Is that enough for this big girl?" Frank asked reverently.

"Ah, we can land in about 3300 feet," He said. "It's really getting back up which will be fun."

"How much do you need?" Frank looked worried.

"Piece of cake," the General lied. "I've taken off in 4700' before, and we'll be light. Only four pax, two crew, and we won't take on any fuel. We'll have 20 minutes to spare after the short hop to Lubbock so we'll do fine."

Patrick and Sharon had been snuggled in the corner of the bench in the rear of the cabin since before take-off and Frank kept casting them furtive glances. "Those two," he said. "You'd think angels would show a little more decorum."

"Oh, Cassiel and Adriel vacated before we got on the plane," Clara corrected. "That's all Sharon and Patrick."

Surprise lit Frank's face. "Patrick McElroy, the confirmed bachelor? Well who would have guessed?"

"And Sharon tells me she has a new-found resolve in connecting with wayward students after her exposure to the angelic way of thinking," Clara followed up. "She's even excited for school to start again on Monday."

"Monday? What day is today?" Frank asked, looking puzzled.

"It's Saturday, Frank. This whole chain of events has only taken 36 hours," Clara said.

Frank just shook his head in wonder.

DANIEL WAS SITTING with the Palehorse squad, deep in conversation.

"Man, if I had the youth I'd be back over there tomorrow," Kettlebell was saying.

"Me too," added another of the four.

"Ditto," chimed in the third. "How about you Gunny? Wouldn't you go back if you could?"

"I am going back," Gunny replied.

"Say what?" all three of his troops called at once.

"Yep, the General has a new contract for personal security team training in country and he's asked me to head it up," Gunny told them. "He'd been thinking about it for a while and this trip made up his mind."

"Well crud Gunny, where does that leave us?" Kettlebell asked.

"Doesn't leave you anywhere unless you choose not to come along," Gunny replied, cracking a huge grin.

"Yeehaw," called one of the others. "Back in the thick of it."

"There'll be some action, I'm sure," Gunny offered. "But we're really going to be teaching youngsters how to protect their primary without getting killed in the process."

"How about you squid?" Kettlebell asked Daniel.

Daniel smiled at the friendly jab. "I'm thinking I need to go see my old CO and find out if he has a place for me on a team," he replied thoughtfully. "I hadn't realized how much I miss the action."

"Well if your CO doesn't make a place for you he's any idiot," Gunny replied. "And you just come see me. Pays a lot better, living conditions a damn sight better, and you'll get to use what Uncle Sam taught you to help a lot of newbies stay alive."

CLARA WAS SMILING AT Frank, just holding his hand and looking at him when her eyes flared brilliant white again. "Father was not easily convinced I was correct in my assessment but I finally won him over," she said without preamble. "He looked at all the possibilities and decided it was worth the risk of his direct interaction."

"I'm sorry Raquel, but I don't know what you're talking about," Frank admonished.

"I have convinced my Father to restore Clara to full health," she replied simply.

Frank was stunned into silence. After several attempts he finally opened his mouth and words actually came out. "What does Clara have to say about this? Will she retain her abilities? *I'm* not concerned about that but *she* puts a great deal of stock in her ability to find missing children."

"Her abilities will remain, she has earned them," Raquel said. "Once I explained to Father that there have been four occasions where her will power was all which kept me from being expelled and her body destroyed, He realized just how strong she really is."

"So what now?" Frank asked expectantly.

"Now," Raquel said simply.

The light in Clara's eye extinguished and Clara's smile for Frank was beatific. "Now you can help me up, dear," she said, extending her hand.

Frank rose from his seat, bracing his head against the top of the cabin and reaching both hands for his wife's. She rose slowly, a little unsteadily, but soon stood fully erect, her face upturned to beam into her husband's gaze.

"Aren't you going to kiss me?" His wife asked.

THIRTY-SIX

"DARLING, HAVE YOU SEEN my car keys?" Clara called to Frank. "I want to take a trip down to the market for some fresh fish for dinner," she said. A soft beeping came from the table by the front door.

"Thank you, Frank. I keep forgetting you put that locator fob on them."

"For a woman who can find a missing child with only their picture you sure do have trouble with your keys," Frank said, walking up behind her and burying his nose in her hair at the nape of her neck.

Sighing, she turned her head to expose more of her neck and he nuzzled hungrily. "Are you sure you need to go anywhere?" he asked provocatively.

"Frank, I swear since I've been healed, you are insatiable," she laughed. "I'll be back in half an hour and there'll be time for that before dinner." Then she froze, going rigid.

"What is it?" Frank blurted, concern painting a portrait of fear across his ruggedly-handsome features.

"Yes I can hear you, Priscilla," she said to thin air.

Frank moved around in front of Clara, looking deeply into her eyes. He was thinking stroke, Transient Ischemic Aneurism, possession? But Clara's eyes were clear and she patted his arm reassuringly.

"Yes dear, I'll make sure he knows. Thank you," she said. It sounded like listening to one end of a telephone conversation. Clara relaxed and Frank moved her to the sofa a few feet away.

"What was that?" he asked, near panic on his face.

"That was a parting gift from Raquel," she replied. "Apparently I can now have telepathic conversations with certain people who have been vessels for angels."

"So, that was actually Priscilla?" Frank said, amazed.

"Yes, and she wanted me to let you know she's on a hunt in western Pennsylvania with Marston and Kristine. They're closing in on two demons who apparently came through the portal and succeeded in finding hosts," Clara explained.

"They caught a third and Kristine used a power phrase to command it to reveal all it knew."

Looking frightened, she rose, turning to stare into her husband's eyes. "It told them there were over a hundred who achieved permanent status here and they're spreading out. They haven't forgotten their mission and they're trying to start movements with any groups willing to participate. A neo-Nazi group in Pittsburg is suspected of having several members who have demonic riders. Hamilton tracks them from his side of the veil and when he comes to visit," she stopped, blushing.

"What?" Frank asked, exasperated.

"They're so young, Frank," she said smiling. "We're you ever desperately in love at fourteen?"

"Yeah, I remember my first crush at fourteen but it was nothing like what I saw in those two. But why was she contacting you?" Frank asked warily. "Was she just reaching out to let us know she was doing well?"

"Oh, no dear, nothing as simple as that," Clara shook her head. "She reached out because, my love, I have to help her find the ones that are heading for Oklahoma."

FINI (?)

Don't miss out!

Visit the website below and you can sign up to receive emails whenever J. Don Wright publishes a new book. There's no charge and no obligation.

https://books2read.com/r/B-A-OIJJ-VKSDB

BOOKS 2 READ

Connecting independent readers to independent writers.

About the Author

J. Don writes young adult science fiction when he's not busy teaching college classes or helping his students and grandchildren work through tough life decisions. He proudly wears a T-shirt which reads, "The people I care about the most call me Papa."